I0761031

The Unseen Soul

Book 1: Immortals

Dale Irwin

Chapter 1

A man with tan skin and black hair hacked at a massive tree as the wind began to pick up. With one final swing, the tree began to fall, only for a sudden gust of violent wind to catch it and blow it the opposite way, right on the woodcutter. Screaming in fear, he tried to turn but tripped over a root and fell. He covered his head and braced himself, waiting for the impact. After a moment, he opened his eyes. A young white man with silver hair and bright green eyes stood off to the side with a hand raised. The tree and his hand were both outlined in a glowing blue energy.

"Are you just gonna sit there, or are you gonna move?" the silver-haired young man asked.

The man with the black hair quickly scrambled to his feet and ran as the tree lowered to the ground.

"You saved my life, Gaius. Thank you," he said, bowing.

"Get back to town, Forest. I'll take it from here," Gaius told him, turning his attention to the tree.

"Um, yes, sir," Forest replied before heading into the woods.

Gaius stared at the tree for a second.

Damn thing's like fifty feet, he thought. *There's no way he'd have been able to get to the town.*

Gaius raised a hand and summoned a line of blue spectral swords at each meter of the tree. He clenched his fist, causing all of the swords to swing down and cut the tree to pieces. With a quick flourish of his hand, the pieces became encased in blue energy and flew up into the air, hovering over Gaius' head.

Pretty sure this is the right size. If not, I can grab another.

Gaius began his trek back to town when he heard a scream. Quickly following the sound, Gaius found Forest pinned down by a massive lion-like creature with a scorpion tail.

Breathing out an annoyed sigh, Gaius swung his hand, and a tree to the right of the manticore exploded, sending piercing wooden shrapnel into the creature's hide. It screamed in a voice that wasn't quite human as the force threw it from on top of Forest. Forest was unharmed and took off, scrambling to the south. The manticore leapt to its feet and was about to give chase until Gaius flicked his wrist and ripped the wooden shrapnel out through the manticore's face, exploding its head like a watermelon.

Gaius proceeded forward, careful to avoid stepping in the viscera and ruining his shoes, and followed the direction of Forest.

In five short minutes, he emerged from the woods and was standing before a small town with wooden thatched roof huts and the beginnings of a stone wall around it. Women and children were wandering the streets, going about their day as men were busy patrolling or working on placing the massive stones where the front gate would be.

Wind Swept Village was rather small, with only a population of about a hundred people, but it had plenty of space for everything. There was a mead hall towards the back that served as both the town hall and home to the chief and his family. A farm took up three acres to the east, which was tended to by various people, while also having the only well in town that connected to an underground river.

The town center, if it could be called that, consisted of a few stalls where people would trade for various things encircling a large fire pit that was dug roughly a meter into the ground, only to be used for festivals.

A tall man in his late forties with tan skin, tribal tattoos up his arms and short black hair was talking with Forest by the makeshift wall. He caught sight of Gaius and waved him over. Gaius obliged, dropping the logs down as he did so.

"There you are, Gaius. Forest was just telling me how you saved his life twice today," he said.

"It's what I do," Gaius replied with a shrug.

"Quite. Well, regardless, we are grateful to you once again. Your telekinesis is truly a gift from the gods," the man replied.

"Chief Thunder, I'm going to rest for today, if you don't mind," Forest explained, with a bow.

Chief Roaring Thunder replied with a nod, not looking away from Gaius. Forest Walker nodded and headed into the village.

"So... Care to explain why you were out there without my permission?" Thunder asked.

"I was... sleepwalking?" Gaius replied.

"You're wide awake."

"I could've woken up in the woods."

"Bullshit."

"It's not. Honest."

"Tell me the truth, or else." Thunder raised a hand as electricity sparked between his fingers.

"All right, geez. I was bored. I wanted something to fight," Gaius grumbled.

Thunder stared at him for a second before shaking his head with a sigh.

"Gaius, you need to get this lust for battle under control. It's going to become a problem in the future if you can't."

Gaius didn't answer him, merely looking at the ground. Thunder sighed and started to head into town.

"Come on. Tala's got dinner cooking, and we need to talk about tomorrow," Thunder said.

Gaius didn't reply but followed after him. They walked through the village, heading towards the mead hall. Thunder kept a strong lead as they walked, while Gaius walked with his head down.

Even without reaching out to his mind, Gaius could tell what Thunder was thinking. Thunder had tried many times in the past to help Gaius pull his desire for conflict under control, but nothing ever seemed to work.

In truth, Gaius didn't fully understand why he felt such a strong urge to battle. There was a strange drive in him, a hollow feeling that his life was meant to be more than it currently was, that *he* was more than he actually was. He didn't know what he was meant to be, but he knew it couldn't be this. He wasn't meant to spend his life in a small village, constantly struggling against the endless tide of monsters and demons from the forest. He had psychic power greater than anyone had ever seen. He had to have been given this power for a reason, right?

Lost in his thoughts, Gaius almost walked into Thunder's back as he was opening the door to the mead hall. The hall was two stories, with the upper level acting as the home for the Chief of the tribe. There was a set of massive oak tables long enough to fit the whole village. There was a raised platform on one end by the stairs that sat a wooden throne, as well as a few barrels along the side that housed different fruits and breads. When Thunder brought Gaius here the first time, he told Gaius that the original village Chief, Thunder's great-grandfather, won a bet with a Viking, and as payment, the Viking built this mead hall for the village. Gaius followed Thunder as they headed up the stairs and entered a small living room section with a set of chairs around a stone hearth, a long hallway leading down to the four bedrooms, and a doorway that led into the small kitchen.

"You're unusually quiet. Something on your mind?" Thunder asked.

"Not really," Gaius replied, still not looking up.

"Bullshit," Thunder said.

Gaius didn't reply.

"What, are you two fighting again?" a voice asked behind them.

Gaius looked up to see a young woman with tan skin and waist-long black hair. She had deep brown eyes and wore loose clothes with a floral pattern on them.

"Come on, cheer up. You're really annoying when you get all mopey," she said, pinching Gaius' cheek.

Gaius pulled away and shook his head.

"Stop it, Tala, geez," Gaius grumbled.

"Tala, Gaius and I were hoping you'd join us for a conversation," Thunder explained, placing a hand on her shoulder.

"Huh?" Gaius asked.

"Oh? Suddenly, you want to talk? Come, take a seat," Thunder said, sitting down and gesturing Gaius forward.

Gaius stared on in confusion as Tala sat down next to him. Scratching his head, Gaius sat at the table across from them.

"So, what's going on?" Gaius asked.

"There's something we wanted to talk to you about. Five years ago, when we brought you here, I know that you took an immediate liking to my little Tala," Thunder began with a smile.

Gaius' face turned bright scarlet, causing Tala to chuckle.

"I... um... uh..." Gaius stammered.

"Come on, you think no one noticed? You tailed me like an excited little puppy," Tala chuckled.

Gaius' eyes widened and immediately darted back to Thunder.

"Relax, it's okay. Truth be told, Eros' aim is true for both of you," Thunder explained.

"Wait, what?" Gaius asked, extremely confused.

"Tomorrow is your birthday. You're becoming a man, a man with the potential to be a great leader. However, every man needs... a little something to bring him under control. For most men, the love of a great woman is enough to keep them on track. That's why I want you to take Tala's hand, and become the next Chief of Wind Swept Village," Thunder continued.

Gaius' heart leapt into his throat, pounding with joy, only to immediately sink into a deep dark pit. He loved Tala; that was truer than anything else in the realms, but he also felt empty inside.

He took a deep breath and blew it out through his nose. "I was planning on leaving tomorrow."

The air in the room changed. Thunder and Tala looked at him, surprised and concerned.

"Why?" Tala asked.

Gaius scratched his head and paused for a second to think before he spoke. "I don't have any memories of my life before you found me. I don't know who I am, where I came from, or who I'm supposed to be, and I won't find that out here. My psionic abilities are stronger than most people's magic, and there has to be a reason for it, right? That can't just be some kind of fluke."

Gaius looked pleadingly at Tala and Thunder. They sat for a moment in silence, until Thunder nodded.

"I understand," he said.

"Really?" Tala and Gaius asked.

"Gaius, it isn't unusual to feel the way you do. Everyone wants to know what they're supposed to do with their life at some point, and not everyone will find it where they've spent their life to that point. Fate works in mysterious ways," Thunder explained.

"Are you... Are you planning on coming back?" Tala asked.

Her eyes were glistening with tears, and she was rubbing her arrowhead necklace. Gaius knew that she was trying to keep her emotions— and by extension, her magic— in check. Thunder pulled her into a hug and kissed his daughter on the top of her head.

"Truth be told, I was wondering the same thing," Thunder said.

"Well, you guys are my family, and of course, I'd love to spend my life with you, Tala. I wasn't planning on staying away forever, even less so now. If I come back after a few months, then we can still get married and help run the village," Gaius explained.

"How long though?" Tala asked.

Gaius thought for a second before responding. "I guess a month, maybe two. If I can't figure something out, then maybe it'll be a sign that I should be here."

"Two months would give us time to plan a wedding," Thunder added.

"Is that okay?" Gaius asked Tala.

Tala seemed to be lost in her own thoughts, absentmindedly rubbing her necklace. Gaius' question brought her back to reality, and she responded. "I guess two months isn't that long. I just... Wish you didn't have to go alone."

Tala got to her feet and started towards the kitchen. Gaius jumped up and followed her.

"Hey, it's my day to cook, right?" He asked with a smile, desperate to try and improve her mood.

She put up a hand to stop, hitting him in the chest and not making eye contact.

"It's fine," she said softly. "I don't mind cooking today."

Gaius stepped back for a second, watching her go into the kitchen. He turned to Thunder, who shook his head.

"Just give her some time. I'm sure this is really hard for her. Having someone you love leave isn't easy," Thunder said, getting up and heading over to a nearby cabinet.

He opened it and pulled out three mugs and a bottle of mead. He returned to his seat a minute later with them filled with mead. He set down one for himself and one for Gaius, with the third next to him for Tala. Gaius looked towards the kitchen before returning to his seat across the table.

"So, where are you going first?" Thunder asked.

"Well, the stories of heroes always start from the beginning, so I figured that's what I'd do," Gaius replied.

"Falling Star Lake, then?"

"That's about as early as I know."

"I see. Mind if I ask you why you decided on this so suddenly?"

"It's just... Something that's been on my mind lately."

Tala entered with plates of food, ranging from fish to pork.

"Dinner time," she announced.

The three sat and began to eat. As Thunder and Gaius talked, Tala absentmindedly picked at the fish on her plate. Gaius watched her silently, and contemplated reaching out to her mind, but thought better about it.

Maybe Thunder's right. Maybe she just needs some time.

Thunder also seemed to notice his daughter's more reserved attitude, and stopped trying to press for a conversation. After a few minutes of silence and eating, Thunder finished eating and got up, stretching and yawning as he did so.

"We should get some sleep. Tomorrow's a big day for us," he said.

"Yeah, that's probably for the best," Gaius said.

Thunder headed for his room, leaving Gaius and Tala to clean the table.

"So, you were kinda quiet tonight. Everything okay?" Gaius asked.

"I just don't get it. Why do you wanna leave here? This village has been your home for five years, and you were just going to leave without any warning," Tala explained, her voice quaking.

"That's not true," Gaius replied.

"Really? Then why is today the first time we've heard anything about it? I'm supposed to be your best friend. You claim that you love me, and yet you were just going to walk away."

"I just... didn't want to hurt you."

"Yeah, because I would've been totally fine with you just walking away without even a good-bye. Did you ever think to, I don't know, talk to me about it? Maybe I would've wanted to go with you."

"You can't."

"Why the fuck not?!"

"I have to do this alone. I'm sorry, but this is the only way I'll be able to figure myself out."

Tala's eyes filled with tears, and she pushed Gaius out of the way and ran to her room.

"Way to go, dumbass," Gaius muttered to himself.

Using his telekinesis, he was able to clean everything up in roughly fifteen minutes before retiring to his own room. Though he wasn't tired, he laid down in his dark room and stared at the ceiling. He stayed like that for a minute until something in his mind screamed at him that he wasn't alone. Bolting straight up in bed, he saw a shadow move across his wall, before suddenly losing consciousness.

Gaius didn't dream too often, but when he did, it was always the same. He found himself standing before a massive stone castle. The structure was solid, standing like a massive monolith of power. Looking around, Gaius could see the incredible branches of the World Tree. This castle rested at its crown, and Gaius could see all nine realms below. There was a grinding sound as the gates opened, and the interior revealed itself to him. The inside was dark, but Gaius could see a golden throne resting on a platform at the end of a long hall.

He began to walk forward, unsure if he was being compelled to or doing it of his own free will. As he walked, light poured inside the castle. He looked around and saw gods and goddesses around. The Olympians, the Aesir, the Vanir, the Palace of Heaven, and dozens of others he had never met all stood on opposite sides of a long red carpet. He watched them as he walked, and they all smiled before dropping to a knee, the way one does before a king.

Gaius got to the throne and climbed the steps to it before stopping. He turned around and the castle walls were gone. Before him stood millions of people from different races. Elves, fae, dwarves, centaurs, humans, demons and gods all stood staring up at him. Gaius felt a hand on his shoulder and turned to see an Indian man with elongated earlobes and whose hair was done in waves and tied into a knot on the top of his head wearing monk robes, step from behind the throne.

The Buddha bowed low and took Gaius' hand before placing a kiss on it. He rose back to standing and pulled a golden crown encrusted with diamonds, rubies, and emeralds and proceeded to place it on Gaius' head. He stepped back and gestured for the throne. Gaius sat down on the throne as the Buddha bowed down again.

"Gaius..." a voice whispered from behind the throne.

Gaius jumped in surprise, but the dream remained.

"This is your birthright. You know it to be true. Just reach out... and take it," the voice whispered as cold hands placed themselves on his shoulders.

Gaius tried to turn his head but found it impossible. He could only move his eyes frantically and catch a glimpse of the hands topped with long, dark nails that seemed to hold him in place. The subjects below him all looked up, and he could see the hollow, empty eyes. Their faces flickered in and out as they began to march forward. This part of the dream was new, and terrifying. It usually ended when he sat on the throne, but now he wasn't sure what was happening. Was he under attack? Had he crossed a god of sleep somehow? What was happening?

"Realize the truth," the voice rasped.

Gaius tried to close his eyes, but found them unwilling to cooperate as the entities drew closer. He tried to scream, tried to move, but was utterly paralyzed. The entities made it to the top and drew into the throne.

Blue fire came next.

Blazing heat, the likes that Gaius had never felt, rushed towards the throne and singed away the dream entities in a flash of blue. The voice released a violent hiss as its hands sizzled and burnt, causing it to release Gaius. The fire spun around the throne, not damaging Gaius, and causing whatever it was behind the throne to scream in agony. Gaius leapt to his feet and spun around to look behind the throne, only to see a body writhing in agony and burning with bright blue flames rolling around on the floor.

"You bastard! You bastard!" it screamed.

Gaius wasn't sure if it was the heat or the light of the fire, but something was making it impossible to make out exactly what it was.

"You shouldn't be here," a second voice came from behind Gaius.

Gaius was frozen for a split second as the voice donned on him.

"Wait!" he yelled in the same voice, trying to face the new arrival.

There was the sound of snapping fingers, and Gaius awoke with a start. Acting quickly, he jumped up and summoned a long, slender sword of blue psychic energy. The sword cast a pale blue light over everything, revealing his room to be empty. He was revealed by this, but only slightly. Dispersing the sword, he laid back down in his bed and surrounded his mind with a barrier of psychic energy before closing his eyes. This time, sleep took longer to find him.

Chapter 2

The next morning, Gaius woke up early and started to pack everything he needed into a large knapsack before heading down while everyone was asleep. He exited their small housing section into the main mead hall, and was greeted by Tala.

"Tala! Good morning," Gaius said in surprise.

"I knew you were gonna try and leave without saying goodbye," she replied dryly.

"No, that's not—" Gaius began.

"Save it. As much as I don't wanna see you go, I know there isn't anything I can do to try and stop you. There is one thing I wanted to do, though," Tala cut him off while pulling out something from her pocket.

She held out her hand, and in its palm was a small flint arrowhead. There was a hole drilled through the part that connected to the arrow, with a piece of string through it.

"Your necklace?" Gaius asked, puzzled.

"Put your hand under mine," Tala instructed.

Gaius recognized what she was doing and did as he was told. She took the string and wrapped it around their hands.

"Swear to me that in two months' time, you'll return to the village, no matter what," Tala instructed.

"I swear," Gaius answered.

The string of the arrowhead began to glow with a white light as the necklace charm raised into the air as much as it could. A crack of white light suddenly shot up the middle, breaking the arrowhead in half. Tala pulled another string from her pocket and held it over the pieces. One jumped up, and the string wrapped around it before sealing itself to the charm. She handed it to Gaius as she put the other half in her pocket.

"There. This charm is linked to mine. If you ever feel lost, all you need to do is hold it out, and it will guide you to me," Tala explained as Gaius put it on.

"Wow, thank you," Gaius said.

They stood in silence for a second before Gaius finally pulled her into a hug.

"I know you're worried, but I'll be okay. I promise," Gaius whispered.

"You can prove it by coming back to me," Tala answered.

Gaius lowered his head and took her by surprise as he kissed her.

"How's that for proof?" he asked coyly.

"Yeah, well... You're still leaving, so don't think this makes it better," she stammered back.

Gaius put on his necklace and headed out the door as Tala watched silently. The sun was starting to rise, but no one was out yet, leaving the small town eerily silent. Gaius walked through the town, taking a second to look around and reminisce.

The feeling of homesickness and nervousness hit him right in the gut as he approached the town gate that was almost done being built. As he looked back at the village where he had spent the last five years, his heart grew heavier as he briefly contemplated whether he should leave or not.

This is your birthright.

The memory of the dream shot into Gaius' mind and sent a cold shiver down his spine. He realized he needed to go. He needed answers. He just wasn't sure if he'd be ready for them. Turning his back to his home, he headed into the forest, towards Falling Star Lake.

He headed north and arrived at the lake within the hour. There used to be a town on the shores, but all that was left was overgrown ruins. As he walked through the ruins of the town, he came upon the large empty plot with several dozen stones aligned in rows. Gaius bowed his head for a minute and offered up a small prayer for the dead, even though he knew that their souls had long been put to rest. He walked through the ruins, scanning everything he saw and trying to find any sort of clue to point him in any direction at all, when he saw something move out of the corner of his eye.

"Um... Hello?" Gaius called out, coming to a stop.

The only answer was an ominous wind that swept through the ruins, screaming like dead souls.

I don't think I should be here. Something feels... wrong. Gaius thought to himself.

He turned to leave, but was stopped when he heard chanting coming from the direction the lake was in.

"I know this is a bad idea, but I should probably go check that out," Gaius said to himself.

He headed deeper into the ruins and emerged on the shores of a massive lake that had to be no less than a kilometer in diameter. Standing on the shore and chanting out a hymn in a language he didn't know, was an old woman who supported herself on a cane. She was wearing a robe that was as gray as her hair, and barely came up to Gaius' chest in height. Her back was to him, but Gaius felt like she was watching him.

"Um... Excuse me, what are you doing here? It isn't safe. Monsters have been seen roaming these ruins, they could attack you if you aren't careful," Gaius called out to her.

The old woman continued with her hymn as if he said nothing at all. Gaius became frustrated by this and called out again: "Come on, stop playing around. Are you deaf?"

The old woman finished her hymn and turned to face him. Her hair covered her eyes, but Gaius could feel the intensity as she stared at him without saying anything for a couple of seconds.

“So, uh, what hymn were you singing?” Gaius asked, fidgeting under her gaze.

“A hymn to the gods of death, wishing these souls a peaceful death,” she rasped. Her voice sounded ancient, like she had witnessed the creation of time itself.

“A peaceful death? It’s been five years, I’m sure they're already resting peacefully,” Gaius said, looking around.

“Five years for you, perhaps. For some, it may only have been yesterday,” She wheezed in response.

“Um... Okay. What are you doing out here, by yourself?” Gaius asked.

“In truth, I was waiting for you, Gaius,” She answered, shifting her head away from him.

“Wait, you know me?” Gaius asked, confused.

“Yes. I’ve known you for a long time, and I’ve waited for this for many moons,” the old woman began to draw a circle in the sand with her staff.

“That’s great! Can you tell me who I am? What am I supposed to do with my life? What’s my name? Did I have a family? Anything?” Gaius stammered excitedly.

“So many questions for one so young,” the old woman responded.

“Well, yeah. Waking up on this beach as the village burned around me is the earliest I can remember. Surely there’s something you can tell me,” Gaius became increasingly more excited and began to pace back and forth.

“Of course. I have the answers to your questions, but I can’t tell you them,” she began to draw stick figures in the circle as Gaius paced.

“What?” Gaius stopped in his tracks and stared daggers into the old woman.

“Unfortunately, child, it is not time for you to learn the answer to these questions,” the old woman replied.

“What does that mean?!” Gaius yelled.

"The answers you seek will come in time. You only need to be patient. Today, my goal is simply to send you on your way," she responded.

"And how are you gonna do that?" Gaius snapped in response, visibly frustrated.

She tapped her staff on the ground outside the circle she drew, bringing Gaius' attention to it. There were three stick figures inside on one side and a giant multi-headed snake-like entity on the other side. Gaius was taken aback, unable to speak or move as a memory he had tried to suppress laid on the sand before him.

"Do you remember now?" the old woman asked.

Despite all his efforts, Gaius never forgot that he caused the death of Tala's mother.

Three miles west of Wind Swept Village is the sea. The village had its own crew of fishermen that used to go there every week before the incident, and people from the village would take their kids to play during the nice weather.

After living with Thunder's family for a year, Tala's mother, a tall, beautiful woman named Wind Walker, had taken them to the beach. The three of them were relaxing on the shore after a long week of helping plant seeds in the village farm. Gaius had closed his eyes for a second when he heard Tala scream.

Bolting straight up, he saw what he first thought was a cluster of sea serpents, until he realized the heads were too closely together. There were eight in total, and all of them were pushing their way to the shore, seemingly approaching the trio.

"Yamata-no-orochi," Wind Walker whispered.

It took a second to fully register what was happening as the massive beast rose out of the water. The eight heads attached to one massive four-legged body, as eight long tails whipped around behind it. The dragon was like a mountain, awe-inspiring in its height, and towered them.

Then, it reared its heads to spew fire...

Gaius reacted first, jumping to his feet and creating a massive blue wall in front of them. Wind seemed to find herself a second later and bolted into action, grabbing Tala as the flames slammed into Gaius' shield with enough force to push him back a few inches, and ran to the forest.

Gaius pushed back against the fire with as much strength as possible, until one of the dragon's legs came up and crushed the barrier while pinning Gaius to the ground. The heads all lowered to inspect their prey, giving Wind enough time to hurl a blast of magic at one of the heads, blinding it in one eye.

The head reared as Wind came running back to free Gaius, but the dragon still had seven heads and eight tails. With agility unlike anything its size should have, Yamata clenched its claw around Gaius and spun incredibly fast, whipping its tails around and smacking them into Wind's torso. The breaking bones and her scream were the last thing Gaius remembered from that day as he blacked out shortly after.

He remembered hearing voices as he started to come to. Thunder was talking to the town healer, and Gaius could only pick up the end of their conversation.

"What do you think?" Thunder asked.

"I think..." The doctor took a deep breath before continuing, "...I think she was too close to the epicenter of that explosion. She's lucky she wasn't completely destroyed by it, but the force mangled her body. I don't think she'll be pulling through this one."

There was silence for a second.

"You think Gaius caused that explosion, don't you?" Thunder asked.

"He's the only one who could've," the healer replied.

Thunder didn't say anything in response.

"We need to get rid of him," the healer said.

"What?" Thunder snapped.

"We don't know what this boy is capable of, and on behalf of my mangled sister, I can firmly say that this boy is nothing but trouble. Think about the state of Falling Star Village when you found him. Do you want our home to end up looking like that too?"

"That won't happen."

"How can you be sure?"

"Because I think we found him for a reason."

"What reason exactly?"

"I don't know, but think about it. He just destroyed Yamata-no-orochi with a release of his power. The only other person to achieve such a feat was Susanoo, and it wasn't even a fight. He's gotta be some kind of demigod or something, maybe his destiny requires that we keep him and raise him."

"What about Tala, then?"

"She can never know what happened. Neither of them can. Promise me that."

"But—"

"Promise me that," Thunder emphasized the words sternly.

A moment of silence followed his words, until Gaius heard the door open. Keeping his eyes closed, Gaius could hear sniffling and sobbing.

"Tala?" Thunder asked.

Gaius took this chance to slowly open his eyes. Though the light blinded him, he could see Tala standing there at the door crying. Without a word, she raced across the room, threw her arms around Thunder and began to sob. Gaius sat up and met Thunder's eyes. There was no malice there, only a deep, profound sadness. Forcing himself to his feet as his body screamed its protest, Gaius wrapped his arms around the two and was immediately hit with a blast of emotion powerful enough to leave permanent scars on his mind.

From Tala, he felt the awful, deep sadness that can only come from losing a parent. The deep, hollow impact that tears away a chunk of your soul and changes who you are at a fundamental level. Thunder's mind was wracked with a similar sadness, but more heavily so with guilt than anything else. He felt guilty that he hadn't been there, guilty that we couldn't save the woman he loved from this fate, and guilty that he couldn't have saved his daughter from this pain. These were emotions that Gaius had never felt. They reached deep inside his mind and fed the emotion he was feeling the most then: anger.

Damn it, he thought. *This is my fault. I...*

No, Thunder's voice echoed through his head. *Our fates are written by the gods, they decide how we live our lives.*

Gaius didn't realize he had forgotten to close his mind before thinking, but he welcomed the company.

Why would they allow this to happen? Gaius asked in response.

They don't care about us. We are toys for their amusement.

Gaius blinked away tears as the memory flashed through his mind.

"You realize it now, don't you?" the old woman asked.

"Am I... a demigod?" Gaius asked.

There was a moment of pause as the old woman seemed to ponder the question.

"You are what you choose to be. Your origins do not define you or your capabilities," she replied.

"That doesn't answer my question."

"It will."

"What is it with you oracles and being vague and confusing? Does it come with the job, or do the gods just tell you to do it to fuck with people?"

"You aren't meant to know—"

"Then what am I meant to know?! All you've done is given me vague bullshit answers and drudge up a memory I'd rather leave forgotten!" Gaius' temper flared, agitated by the lack of help the old woman had offered him.

The old woman thought for a second before answering, "You're right, ask your questions, and I'll do my best to answer within my power."

"'Within your power'? What does that mean?" Gaius asked, confused.

"There are... Entities that would rather this conversation go in a specific... Direction, as it were," the old woman explained.

Her choice of words and small pauses gave Gaius an uneasy feeling.

"Um... Okay, I guess. You said you know me. Does that mean you know my name?" he asked carefully.

"Your name is Gaius. Gaius Vinces," she replied.

A feeling of strength resonated through Gaius' body. Names could hold great power, and losing your name could cause an emptiness in your soul that could keep you from truly understanding yourself. Gaius smiled as the strength washed through him, filling him with a warmth he had never known.

"What is your next question?" the old woman asked.

"Um... Right. What happened here five years ago? What destroyed this village?" Gaius asked.

"A battle. Two brothers went to war with each other, and this village was caught in the middle. It was unfortunate, but unavoidable."

The words struck a chord in Gaius. He felt something tugging at his subconscious.

"Was I here?" he asked.

"Yes."

"What happened to me?"

"I can't say."

"What are those entities you were talking about?"

"I can't say."

"Are they gods?"

"They're more than that."

"What?"

Lightning flashed overhead and thunder roared like a dragon.

"You should probably move on from this topic," the old woman said.

"Um... Okay. Where do I go from here?"

"Now you're asking the right question. If you've been paying attention, you should be able to figure it out."

"Paying attention? What—?"

This is your birthright.

The dream flashed through Gaius' mind again. The throne was placed above all the gods, the Buddha himself knelt before him, and he was crowned king.

"No. No, that doesn't make any sense. I can't be destined to become a god. I'm just... Just..." Gaius stammered, staggering back.

"Just what? Just a man who destroyed Yamata-no-Orochi by accident? Just a man with the ability to read minds, move objects with his mind, and destroy beasts without hesitation or effort? Destiny is destiny, Gaius. Your destiny is what brought you here, what brought me here today. Your life, your *existence*, is a sign of great change. The realms are about to be thrown into chaos, and it will be because of the actions *you* take. Even if you try to avoid it, there's a force greater than you that is going to take you where you need to go. A man often finds his fate on the road he takes to avoid it, but with a much worse result," the woman explained, a hard edge to her voice.

The two stood in silence for a minute while Gaius reeled at the thought. What did any of this mean? How could his fate affect him so much? He was just one man, he might have impressive strength, but to become god was something completely different.

“This can’t be right. Th-Th-There must be a mistake,” Gaius stammered.

“I doubt you believe that,” the old woman replied.

“Of course I do. It’s the only thing that makes any sense.”

“Denial will get you nowhere.”

“We’ll see about that,” Gaius turned to leave.

“Where are you going?” the old woman asked.

The question stopped Gaius in his tracks. He honestly didn’t have an answer, so he simply replied, “Away from you.”

An image raced through his mind of a set of hands reaching out to try and grab the outstretched hand of a man with long red hair while another man with gray hair and an eyepatch loomed behind him before putting a spear to the other man’s throat. The image was filled with pain and terror that brought Gaius to his knees.

Before he could react, he saw another image rip through his mind. This one was someone in a pool of water with a fruit tree hanging over him. He couldn’t drink or eat, and his stomach was overcome with ravenous hunger and thirst. It was filled with pain and rage. Gaius grabbed his head as he fell face first in the sand. He tried to scream, but his throat wouldn’t respond as the two images flashed back and forth.

“The pain you’re feeling is the pain inflicted by gods. Your destiny is to fix this. You are the chosen one, blessed with the power and destiny to alter the minds of all gods,” the old woman explained, walking forward.

She stopped in front of Gaius as he writhed on the ground and tapped her staff in front of him. The images left his mind without hesitation, and he was finally able to calm down and catch his breath.

“Do you see it now? The worlds live under these gods that would torture, maim and punish anyone they chose. You are going to change that,” she explained as Gaius got to his feet.

“How?” Gaius gasped, still trying to catch his breath.

"There's only one way for you to gain the power necessary to be taken seriously. Think carefully, Gaius," the old woman answered.

Gaius panted until he finally got his breath under control, then looked at the sky as he wracked his mind. Everything she had told him ran through his mind and coalesced into a single thought: "I'm destined to become a god, aren't I?"

A smile passed over the old woman's mouth. She nodded her approval.

"Then, I would need a way to do it, but the Wukong Accords sealed away all the means of it. Except… The ones already used by the gods," Gaius continued, following the train of thought.

"That's right. What would be the closest for you to get access to?" the old woman asked.

Gaius' eyes wandered through the skyline until they rested on the mountain that peeked over the horizon.

"The Olympians use ambrosia to hold onto their power, and Olympus is roughly a three-week trek on land. I could cut it down if I fly," Gaius answered.

"Excellent. Then you should get going. The last thing you want to do is waste time," the old woman replied.

"I don't know, this still doesn't feel right," Gaius scratched his head.

"Following one's destiny never truly does. I bet even Heracles had reservations before he went to King Eurystheus. Yet he completed his trials, he helped the gods battle back the giants, and in the end, ascended to godhood upon his death," the old woman replied, staring at the mountain in the distance.

"Yeah, let's just hope I don't have to die to achieve my destiny," Gaius replied with a smirk.

The old woman said nothing, but the muscles in her hand tensed as she gripped the staff tighter. Her reaction made Gaius even more unsettled than she already did.

"Um... Right, I'm gonna head out now. Thank you for your help, I guess," Gaius said, walking away.

"Wait!" the old woman yelled.

Gaius spun around, confused and nervous, as she approached him again. Her eyes bore into him with an intensity that made his skin crawl.

Then, she wrapped her arms around him and hugged him.

This caught Gaius completely off guard and made him unsure of what to do or say. After a couple of seconds, the old woman pulled back and looked at him.

"You have a long and terrible road ahead of you. There are those who would manipulate and try to destroy you, but you will have friends to watch your back. Keep them safe, and they'll do the same for you," her voice was tinged with sadness that froze Gaius' heart.

The two stared at each other for a minute before Gaius spoke again, "Who are you?"

"Just a helpful hand meant to give you a push," the old woman replied.

The two turned and walked away from each other. Gaius took a quick glance over his shoulder one last time to look at her, but she was gone. He was alone again to ponder all that was said and all that wasn't.

Chapter 3

Tala sat on a log, watching the men of the village construct the wall in utter boredom.

"Sorry I'm late, it took me a minute to find it," a voice said behind her.

She turned to see Thunder, holding a large staff made of finely polished wood, with a golden ring on its tip. A spear tip divided the ring in half, and four separate rings hung freely on either side. Tala's eyes widened when she saw it.

"M-M-Mom's staff," she stammered.

"Not your mother's anymore, it's yours." Thunder said, handing it to her.

Tala got to her feet and took it, feeling the surprising weight when she did.

"Is this...? Am I...?" she asked.

"When she gave birth to you, your mother became incredibly sick. So sick, in fact, we weren't sure she'd make it. She told me that if something were to happen to her, she wanted me to give this to you when you were married. I know it's a bit early, but I figured since you blew up the fourth one this month last week, I'd be doing us all a favor," Thunder said with a chuckle.

Tala felt the tears swell in her eyes as she looked at the staff in her hands. Thunder pulled her in for a hug as she wiped her eyes.

"Take good care of it, okay? I went through a lot to make that for her," Thunder patted her head before she pulled back.

Tala took a second to look the staff over. Though she had seen her mother wield it, she had never held it herself.

"This wood. Ash?" she asked.

"Not just any ash, I carved that from a branch of the World Tree itself," Thunder explained proudly.

"I'm sorry... WHAT?!" Tala yelled in surprise.

"Didn't I ever tell you that story?" Thunder asked.

"I'm pretty sure I'd remember that."

"Hm... Well, when I was in my early twenties, I went on a journey much like the one Gaius is going on now. Over the course of three years, I scaled half of the World Tree and broke off the stick that makes up that shaft. The rings, however, are orichalcum I won in a bet against a pharaoh in Egypt," Thunder explained, nonchalantly.

Tala stared at her father with a look of utter shock on her face.

"What?" he asked.

"My father... Scaled the World Tree and won a bet against a pharaoh?" she replied.

"Of course, I told you I was an adventurer when I was younger."

"Yeah, I just... Didn't expect you to be so... Cool, I guess."

Thunder looked slightly hurt for a second before laughing.

"Anyway, I think this might solve the issue you've been having with your other staves... exploding. Go ahead, cast a spell," he said, patting her shoulder.

Tala nodded and closed her eyes. With a deep breath, she emptied her mind and began to unleash her magic. Her vast reservoir flowed outward and took everything she had to catch it and channel it into the staff.

The large ring began to glow with a brilliant white light as the other rings jumped and jingled in tune. She focused on the staff and could feel her strength barely scratching its depths. She thrust the staff high above her head, spewing an inferno of white hot flames high above her head.

After a second, the fire subsided as everyone in the village looked on in awe. Thunder clapped and cheered in approval as Tala opened her eyes.

"Impressive. With more training, you'll be one of the most dangerous witches of your time!" Thunder exclaimed as the village joined in his applause.

Tala leaned heavy on the staff, panting as her strength slowly began to return.

"That being said, just because you can use your full strength now, doesn't mean you should. This staff won't break, but you still could. You need to control your power usage," Thunder explained, catching his daughter before she could fall over.

"So, why'd you give it to me now? Why couldn't it wait until my wedding?" Tala asked as she caught her breath.

Thunder's face hardened in response to her question.

"You're not going to like my answer," Thunder replied.

"I figured," Tala answered, finding her balance again.

"I got a message this morning from a couple of the nearby villages. A Nucklavee was spotted a few miles south," Thunder said, somberly.

"A Nucklavee?" Tala repeated, surprised.

Nucklavees were demons that were half-man, half-horses. They were destructive to crops and livestock, and hearing even a rumor of one was enough to send small villages like Wind Swept running for the hills. Tala had never encountered one, but she knew how dangerous they were from her mother and father.

"W-W-What do we do? W-What can we do?" Tala stammered.

"First, you can calm down. We don't need your magic running wild again. Second, we need to gather the villagers and start preparing for the worst. We can start an early harvest, pull all the healthy livestock inside, and try to keep everyone indoors for a while. I need you to go into the woods and check our protection wards," Thunder explained.

Though his words carried urgency, he spoke calmingly and with experience only awarded to a man who had been a leader for many years.

Tala, however, was still seventeen, and she had much to learn in the ways of a leader. She was panicking.

"Alone?!? You want me to go out alone?!" She yelled in shock.

"What? Of course not. I'll be sending you out with a party of our best hunters," Thunder replied, calmly.

"Oh. Oh, yeah, that makes sense," Tala sighed, exasperated.

"You should try some breathing exercises, they helped me a lot when I was younger. Wait here while I get everything organized," Thunder chuckled, walking away.

With a wave of his hand, there was an explosion of thunder that echoed through the village. It took roughly two minutes for Thunder to gather a huge crowd in the town center and explain the situation. Immediately, various people headed over to the farm. Others began to round up children and escort them inside. Thunder motioned for four men to join him, and they headed back over to Tala.

"Forest Walker, Silent Wolf, Wild Horse, and Raging River will be accompanying you to the wardstones. We need all four of them checked, I'd recommend starting with the south," Thunder explained.

"Morning, Tala. Where's your boyfriend? Hiding today?" Horse asked.

Tala ignored him and addressed the other three.

"Thanks for helping out. I'm sure I don't need to voice how dangerous this will be. Like Father said, we're heading south. From there, a straight line clockwise, hitting west, north, and finishing east. It should take us no more than two hours tops, stay in a group and stay in the ward. Any questions?" Tala explained her plan in a fast, breathless manner.

Forest raised his hand, and Tala nodded.

"Why would the ward keep away the Nuklavee when it doesn't keep out manticores, chimeras, and that Sidhe from last Hallow's Eve?" he asked.

"A protective ward requires a material that can be used as a conduit, like the ward stones. The material would need to be conductive to magic, but also repel whatever type of creatures you're dealing with. It wouldn't be difficult to make more wards, but I don't have money for all the materials we'd need," Tala explained.

"Maybe you'd have more money if you were engaged to the son of a great trader," Horse muttered.

Tala took a deep breath and, choosing to be the bigger person, walked past the men towards the gate, calling over her shoulder, "Come on, we don't have much time to lose."

It was only a twenty-minute trek to reach the first ward stone, which sat alone in a clearing with a roughly twenty-foot diameter. A large block of quartz that stood over six feet tall sat in the center. There was no visible sign of the ward itself, but the area around the large block pulsed with magic. Tala looked the area over and couldn't see any immediate danger, so she walked over to the stone.

"I'm going to check the ward to make sure the flow hasn't been tampered with. Watch my back," Tala ordered.

It was dead silent as each hunter took a point in one of the cardinal directions. They each faced one another's back so they could see Tala, the woods, and their allies at the same time. Tala placed her hand on the quartz to read its energy pulse. Closing her eyes, she could sense the shape of it. It was a powerful current rushing through the stone. She could recognize the feel of her mother's magic anywhere, and it surprised her that it was still going strong so many years since her passing. Pulling her hand away, she was confident that nothing had tampered with the ward or the stones, but she still wanted to check the other three.

"Regroup, let's head—," Tala began.

She was cut off by a blood-curdling, inhuman, and otherworldly scream. Blood froze in Tala's body as the four hunters tensed in fear and anticipation. A branch broke underfoot of *something* that was much too close for comfort. The five froze, unable or unwilling to move. Tala took a quick scan of their surroundings and realized something she hadn't thought about a minute before.

"River. Get. Your. Ass. In. The. Ward. Now," she growled through clenched teeth.

River refused to face her, but she saw him take note of the danger he was in. He was roughly ten feet from the safety of the ward.

He moved slowly and began to inch closer, until he stepped on a stick that broke under his foot. The break was louder than an explosion in the quiet forest. No one breathed as the seconds stretched on for an eternity.

After a minute that felt like an hour, River continued his journey of a thousand miles. He made it roughly five feet to the stone when a fox came streaking past from the underbrush, yelping and howling as the sound of a galloping horse crashed through the forest.

"RUN, YOU IDIOT!" Tala yelled as she raised her staff.

River took off in a full sprint as the monster crashed into the clearing. It resembled a man on horseback, except that the man and horse were one complete being.

Unlike a centaur, the man's torso rose from the center of the horse, leaving the horse's head untouched. It had no skin, revealing its pink muscle that was stitched with yellow veins. The arms of the man's torso reached the ground and had bizarrely small fins protruding from its wrists.

The human head was three times larger than normal, with sharp white fangs, while the horse head had one eye that shined red like hellfire. It caught sight of River, who screamed in fear and tripped. The creature bounded forward just as Tala thrust her staff forward, releasing a blast of force strong enough to knock her flat on her back.

In her moment of panic, Tala hadn't had a chance to properly orient the spell's strength. While the initial impact didn't destroy the creature, the spell did have enough force to send it careening into the forest, leaving a line of demolition in its wake. The beast was back on its feet a few seconds later and stared down the destruction towards the group who were split in their efforts to drag River, who was dazed from cracking his head on a rock, across the ward and help Tala to her feet.

Rolling its massive head on its shoulders, the human half leaned back and released the same blood-curdling scream they had heard a few minutes before, then proceeded to gallop forward at unbelievable speed.

Despite a gap of at least a hundred feet between them, the nuckelavee was back at the start of the destruction before anyone could think to react. Its long arms shot forward to grab at Forest and Horse, who were trying to help River to his feet. Tala reacted quickly by pulling her staff backwards and causing a wind to grab the three men and blow them forward the last few feet. They tumbled over each other in a groaning pile of tangled limbs as the wind forced them behind the ward just as the nuckelavee's claws slammed into the ground where they were a few seconds before.

The nuckelavee roared in a fury before rushing forward and slamming hard into the ward. In a split second, two things happened. First, the ward exploded in brilliant white sparks and flashed up an incandescent wall between the hunters and the monster. Then, the wall exploded with a force that sent the nuckelavee flying back in a bright white flash. The hunters were blinded momentarily until the flash dissipated.

"What was that?" Horse grunted loudly as he rubbed his eyes.

"The ward repelled the nuckelavee. It can't get any closer," Tala replied, getting to her feet.

After blinking a few times, her sight seemed to even out, letting her see the beast was back on its feet, staring at them. Its head tilted from shoulder to shoulder inquisitively, as if unsure of what happened. Tentatively, it raised an arm and reached forward. Once again, the silver wall of the ward flashed up, repelling its arm away. It didn't seem to hurt the creature, which worried Tala.

If it doesn't get hurt by the ward, the odds are it'll keep trying. I doubt there's any weak spots it could use to break through, but it still could be a problem, she thought to herself.

"What do we do?" Forest asked, breaking himself free from the cluster of bodies on the ground.

Horse and River got to their feet and began to check themselves for injuries. Horse had broken a finger, and River was bleeding from a cut on his head, but there were no serious injuries. Tala never took her eyes off the nuckelavee as it began to pace the clearing.

"It isn't going to leave now," Horse observed.

Tala shook her head in response before turning to Wolf.

"I need you to get my father as fast as you can. Can you do that?" she asked.

Wolf nodded before sitting down cross-legged. He placed his hands in a prayer formation in front of him and closed his eyes. He opened them again and they flashed white momentarily as a spectral white wolf leapt from his body, causing it to fall backwards. The wolf shook its body before asking, "Is there any specific message you wish me to deliver?"

"Tell him the nuckelavee is here and we need his help. Short, simple, sweet. Now go," she replied quickly.

The wolf raced off into the forest, leaving Tala, Horse, Forest and River alone with the creature that wanted them dead.

"So, uh, what do we do now?" Horse asked, barely able to keep the tremble out of his voice.

"The only thing we can do. We wait." Tala replied, sitting down.

"Great. Great. Great," Horse replied, taking a step away from the ward.

Forest and River sat on either side of Wolf's comatose body. Forest picked up a rock and rolled it in his hand before tossing it into the air and catching it. This action seemed to catch the attention of the nuckelavee, because it stopped its pacing and stared directly at Forest. Forest's blood ran cold, but he refused to let it show.

"The fuck you looking at ugly?" he yelled with bravado, and no real brains.

The nuckelavee walked to the ward as close as it could and stared at Forest, before its head went backwards. It began to emit a weird choking-like noise that made its entire body bounce.

"Um... What's it doing?" Forest asked.

"It... It sounds like it's... laughing," Tala replied, genuinely confused.

The mere thought froze the air around them for a handful of seconds before Horse asked the question no one wanted to know the answer to: "What does it have to laugh about?"

Before anyone could respond, the nuckelavee drove its arms into the dirt and flung them up with incredible speed, sending a tidal wave of dirt, rocks, insects and debris hurtling at the hunters. The act was so surprising that all anyone could do was fall over as the air filled with the mess.

Tala didn't have time to cover her face as the initial blast engulfed them, and took a handful of hard rocks to the face, cutting her in several places, and bruising her cheek. Her eyes were too filled with tears and debris to see what happened to the others, but she could hear them yelling and scurrying around. In the confusion, she let go of her staff and rolled over, trying to cover her face and vital organs from the rain of stone. She crawled as fast as she could towards the back of the clearing before getting to the treeline.

She took a few seconds to wipe the dirt, tears, and blood from her eyes before looking for the others. Horse seemed to have crawled into the underbrush in an attempt to hide, while River and Forest had both thought to protect Wolf's body. She scanned the slowly thinning haze of dirt to see if she could see the beast and saw that it had positioned itself near the rubble Tala created when she blasted it earlier. It began to laugh its disgusting choking noise as it leaned over and picked up a fragment of a tree.

Oh shit, Tala thought as she began to jump to the side.

With skill and speed that put to shame even the most skilled spear hunters, it launched the tree fragment at where Tala was hiding. The impact shattered the tree Tala was behind mere moments before. The force of the explosion still caught Tala, and her body screamed in pain as bones broke and splinters like knives ripped into her. She was sent spiraling back into another tree, hitting her head and completely dazing her as a result.

The next few seconds were a blur as she remembered something yelling incoherently. She opened her eyes to see River running to her while Forest pulled Wolf's body to the bush that Horse was hiding in. Then, the air was filled with red as River seemed to explode into a mess of blood and viscera. The look on his face seemed to cry out in pain, but the massive burst of rocks and gravel tore through his chest before the air could leave his lungs.

Tala forced herself to sit up as a new voice began to scream. Willing her mind to focus, she began to shake off the daze as she could finally hear what Forest was screaming.

"... The stone! It destroyed the stone! Tala, can you hear me?!"

Chapter 4

Tala's first thought was to run. The thought screamed in her head as she looked over the mess before her. River's body and the ward stone had been shredded by the first attack, and the silver wall of energy began to fade away. Time itself seemed to slow as the nuckelavee took note of the wall fading.

Then it charged.

Leaping straight over the stone, it crashed down and rushed Tala.

"Tala!" Horse yelled.

His voice seemed like something from miles away, another thing Tala couldn't bring herself to focus on. Slowly, at least to her perception, she fell to her hands and knees. The nuckelavee let out a blood-curdling screech, followed by a massive thud. Tala looked up to see the creature on the ground, covered in vines with sharp thorns that dug into it. It screeched and thrashed, but the vines tightened around it. Something grabbed her arm harshly, yanking her to her feet. Forest brought his hand across her face with a sharp sting, finally snapping her out of the daze.

"Snap the fuck out of it! I know you're scared, but I need you right now. Wolf won't be back for a while. Horse is useless, and my partner is dead! You're all I can count on, so you need to snap to your fucking senses!" Forest yelled at her.

"Yeah, you're right. Sorry," Tala replied, shaking her head.

"Don't apologize, just get your staff before it gets free," Forest replied.

She got to her feet again and faced the nuckelavee, which thrashed against its binds. The horse's head finally began to move as it twisted around and opened its jaw, emitting a black smoke that wilted the vines on contact and caused them to decay. The vines fell away as the nuckelavee leapt to its feet and stared down the two hunters.

"Did you know it could do that?" Forest asked.

"Never faced one before, remember?" Tala took a deep breath to ready herself.

"Yeah, kid, me neither," Forest drew two tomahawks from his waistband and handed one to Tala.

The nuckelavee charged, but Tala wasn't afraid anymore. She focused her magic into the tomahawk and met the creature's arm swing with a white-hot blade of iron that hit its arm. The blade didn't cut the creature, but the heat seemed to singe it and sent its arm reeling.

Forest responded just as quick, raising an arm and summoning a burst of roots that rushed the monster, wrapping around its legs and tripping it. The nuckelavee toppled head over body and landed at the feet of Tala and Forest, who immediately leapt over it and headed towards the ward stone to keep some distance.

As she ran, she caught a glimpse of Horse hiding behind a tree to her right. She had thought that Forest was being harsh when he called Horse useless, but he was right. Here he was, cowering while they fought not just for their own lives, but for the lives of their village as well.

"Coward!" Tala yelled as they ran past.

Horse didn't respond, and Tala didn't care. She grabbed her staff as they ran and turned to face the monster head-on.

"Rip it apart!" Forest yelled as he ran to the quartz.

With her heightened emotions, Tala knew it would be dangerous to call on elemental magic. She also realized she didn't have time to plan something out, as the creature was back on its feet and closing in on her. She acted on instinct more than thought. Pouring her magic into the staff in her right hand, and the tomahawk in her left.

"Sever!" she yelled as she threw the tomahawk with all her might.

It spiraled at the nuckelavee, who leapt high into the air to dodge it. Gripping her staff with both hands, she thrusted it in the direction of the airborne nuckelavee.

Dodge this. She thought, then screamed, "Pierce!"

A spectral blade of magic erupted from the point of the staff, stabbing the nuckelavee in the human torso and sending it flying backwards. It landed in a crumpled mound of flesh, which quickly became entangled in vines that wrapped around. The vines began to grow large oval-shaped pods that began to explode with enough force to embed their seeds in the creature.

The creature began to scream as its horse head was wrapped up in thorny vines that tightened around it. Tala held out her hand as the tomahawk flew back to her. She began to pour magic into the ax as the vines grew around the creature, forcing its arms open to expose its chest.

There was a hole the size of an apple in its chest that oozed black blood. Taking aim, she threw the ax with all her might, hitting her mark with ease. She had pumped so much magic into the ax that it had already begun to break apart in the air. Upon contact, however, the small ax exploded into a blast of shrapnel and energy that ripped into the creature. It thrashed and roared momentarily before collapsing over.

"Is it... Is it dead?" Tala asked.

"I don't know, and I really don't wanna get close enough to find out," Forest replied.

"Either way, let's repair the stone and then get the body outside the ward, just in case," Tala said, looking over to the broken pillar of quartz.

The once grand stone that towered over her now came to her waist, and any remnants of her mother's magic had dissipated. She felt sharp pangs in her chest, knowing that one of the final pieces of her mother were gone from this world, but she still steeled herself for the coming task. She began to walk towards the stone but was stopped as Forest grabbed her shoulder, his face deadly serious. Concerned, she spun to see what he was looking at, and her jaw hit the ground in shock.

The nuckelavee was back on its feet.

The small grasses to the plants Forest had used to contain it had all been laid barren. Both heads were turned towards the gaping chest wound that had exposed the mass of dark goo that seemed to comprise its insides. The creature took an arm and stabbed into the wound, howling as it did so. It ripped out a bone spear the size of a man and tipped with fearsome hooks before the wound sealed itself shut.

"By the gods," Forest whispered.

Before they could react, the monster was airborne, lunging downwards with the spear. Tala threw magic into her staff, creating a dome of energy around them. The spear shattered the dome, sending Tala backwards from the recoil.

Forest was missed by mere inches as the nuckelavee landed, before it swung its free arm at him, catching him in the chest. The crunch of the breaking bones was audible as the wind was knocked clear out of Forest's lungs. He was sent flying past the ward stone, slamming into a tree with another audible break. The impact ripped the tree up from the roots and toppled it over. Tala watched in horror as she became the last hunter willing to fight.

She didn't get time to process it as the beast was in front of her, driving the point of its spear at her face. She barely had time to throw her staff up in defense. The spear hit the staff and sent Tala skidding backwards. She made a mental note to thank her father if she survived this before quickly switching to an offense stance with her staff. She knew she wasn't as experienced as the other warriors in her village, especially not Gaius, but she had enough training to defend herself.

The nuckelavee charged with its spear above its head, and Tala met it with a quick spin and hit the joint in its front right knee. The blow had her entire strength in it, and merely bounced off with an audible *thud.* The nuckelavee reached down and grabbed the staff, yanking it free with ease. It began to pace around Tala, inspecting the staff as it did so. It held the spear out and shook it, causing the rings to rattle before uttering a short version of its choke-like laugh.

It's toying with me, Tala realized.

The creature moved once again with supernatural speed and was behind Tala. She spun to see the tip of her staff coming down quickly, before a spectral white wolf leapt from the forest and slammed its body into the creature's torso. A wave of relief washed over Tala as Wolf bit and clawed at the creature's face and chest. The creature grabbed Wolf by the throat and threw him in the direction of Tala. In midair, the spectral wolf flipped with more grace than it should have and landed beside Tala.

"Are you hurt?" Wolf asked.

"Yes, but I fear Forest has taken a worse beating than me. Did you get to my father?" She replied.

"He's on his way," Wolf replied.

"Did he say how long?" Tala asked.

"It's the chief, it won't be long," Wolf replied, rushing the nuckelavee.

Tala wasn't as fast as Wolf, but she was right behind him. Wolf leapt with jaws open, crunching down on the arm holding Tala's staff. She grabbed the staff as it fell, only for the monster to slam Wolf into her. Wolf yelped in pain, and the air was forced from Tala's lungs in a stifled scream of pain. The nuckelavee loomed over Tala before grabbing and lifting her up by her throat. Wolf leapt again, only to take a spear to the chest. He screamed in pain, then vanished into a puff of smoke that traveled back to his body.

The nuckelavee stared at Tala as she squirmed. Its eyes burned crimson as its jaw began to open. Tala kicked at its chest and tried to break free, but its grip locked around her throat. A tomahawk suddenly flew and hit it in the head, embedding the blade an inch into it.

Tala looked over to see Wolf leaning against a tree with blood oozing from under his shirt. The nuckelavee roared and jumped, turning in midair and hurdling its spear at the same time. Wolf's reactions were faster than Tala, but his chest wound made him sluggish. The spear caught him in his left shoulder, sending him back and pinning him to a tree. He screamed and punched at the spear before trying to pull it out.

The beast landed and went back to trying to eat Tala. Its jaw unhinged more and more and Tala thrashed harder and harder, expending energy she didn't have to try and free herself. After a couple of seconds, she stopped as her body started to reach its limit. The creature's eyes burned into her as it moved her closer. She blinked as the light began to blind her.

Damn, it's like looking at the sun in a mirror. Wait... The thought ran through her head almost too quickly for her to process.

She squinted and saw the light shining from the blade of the tomahawk. She grabbed it and ripped it out, seemingly annoying the nuckelavee as it shook its head. She poured every last drop of magic she could muster into it and held it in front of her.

The blade ignited with white hot fire, then exploded with enough force to send her and the creature flying in two different directions. Hot shrapnel stabbed into her body, and she could feel parts of her body burn as she hit the ground with a bone-breaking thud. The creature was already recovering and reattaching its jaw as Tala forced herself to her feet.

"No. No. Damn it," Tala whimpered.

The creature stared at her for a few seconds, seemingly waiting for her to move. Tala couldn't even bring herself to move, and the creature seemed to understand that. It began to walk towards her before making a quick jump backwards. It repeated the motion every three steps.

"Stop fucking toying with me!" Tala shouted.

The creature uttered its choking laugh in response, but was quickly drowned out by a roar of thunder in the sky. The creature looked up in confusion and, for a second, fear. When it didn't seem to see anything in the sky, it returned its attention to Tala.

C'mon, dad. Hurry, she thought as the nuckelavee finally stepped in front of her.

Lightning struck the ground in front of her, blinding her and sending her falling back in the dirt and landing on her butt. The nuckelavee reared like a horse and screamed in panic. Tala blinked and rubbed her eyes, trying to focus, and managed to regain her sight in a couple of seconds. Her father stood in front of her, with his back to the beast.

"Can you walk?" he asked, holding out his left hand.

Tala didn't respond and only stared in awe at the weapon in her father's hand. She had only seen her father wield it twice, once, humorously enough, to blast a fly that wouldn't leave him alone, and the second time to incinerate a horde of draugr that had made their way too close to the village.

To most, it would look like a bizarre design to a basic club, but Tala knew the story of how her father had won the right to wield by beating its owner in a drum contest. The handle itself had the length of a human arm with the width of a rice bowl, and the tip was topped with a white ball. It was a drumstick belonging to the god Raijin, and it was only used when there was a serious problem.

"Tala, can you stand?" her father asked, snapping her away from her thoughts.

She nodded and took his hand, allowing him to pull her up without resistance. The nuckelavee howled and lunged forward, aiming Tala's staff at the back of Thunder's head. Thunder's reaction was incredible, as he spun in a full circle, bringing his drumstick across the face of the horse, creating an explosion of thunder and lightning that sent the beast flying.

Tala stared in awe as her father completed his motion and faced her once again.

"You did well to hold out for so long, but I'll take it from here. Go tend to the wounded, the healers were right behind me," Thunder ordered.

He was using the same calm voice he was known for using, but his face held the look of a man who was deadly serious. Tala nodded in response and started to limp over to Wolf, who was still pinned to the tree.

"Are you still alive?" Tala asked.

Wolf looked up and smiled, though his complexion was deathly pale, and he seemed ready to faint.

"How bad's your chest?" Tala asked, not sure if she really wanted to see.

Wolf lifted up his shirt to reveal a second stab wound that was oozing blood. It wasn't as deep as the one on his shoulder, but it was still deep enough to be a problem. He looked at her with pleading eyes. Just from the look on his face, she could see his thoughts. *Please don't let me die.*

"I'm gonna send magic into the spear to close the bleeding vessels and dull the nerves. Just hang on, okay?" Tala explained.

Wolf nodded in agreement before turning an evil eye to Horse, who still cowered behind the tree next to them. Tala spat in his direction before placing her hands on the spear and beginning her task.

"To me," Thunder ordered.

Tala's staff flew from the ground by the nuckelavee into his outstretched hand. The nuckelavee screamed in response before bonding to its feet and rushing Thunder. Thunder responded by hitting his drumstick into the ground, sending a column of lightning at the beast. The nuckelavee bounded to one side, dodging the lightning, and raced toward Thunder at full speed.

Closing the gap almost instantly, it swung its arm at Thunder, who tapped the butt of the staff into the ground. Instantly, a dome of translucent light encased Thunder, which the nuckelavee hit with enough force to crack it. The creature swung its other arm, delivering a bizarre flurry from its elastic limbs.

With the dome cracking around him, Thunder brought his two weapons together with a thunder clap. The resulting boom destroyed the dome around him, sending out a wave of broken pieces of light, like shrapnel from a bomb. The force of the attack sent the nuckelavee back with pieces of the magic sticking out of its body, causing it to roar in pain and annoyance.

Thunder tossed his baton into the air and grabbed the staff with both hands. He twirled it quickly, before launching it with all his might at the creature's head. The creature dodged by moving its head, but Thunder's body dispersed into lightning and flew at the spear, coalescing back together next to the staff in the air.

Using his momentum, Thunder grabbed the nuckelavee by the face with one hand, jamming a couple of fingers into its right eye, and the staff with the other before he spun around the creature, landing behind the human torso and violently twisting its neck in the process. With strength beyond a mortal man, Thunder leapt into the air and drove the staff downwards, into the creature's bulbous head.

It screamed in pain before its mouth was abruptly shut by the jaw slamming together as the staff went through them. Thunder drove the staff down until the butt of it stabbed into the horse body and the rings sat at the top of its head, like a bird sitting on a fence post.

He leapt off the creature's back and dispersed into lightning again, zipping back over to catch his baton as it fell. Dispersing once more, he reformed above the creature's head before gripping the drumstick with both hands and driving it down with all his might. He hit the tip of the staff, and the resulting explosion of energy would've been enough to incinerate the entire clearing if he hadn't. The staff absorbed the lightning and dispersed it into the nuckelavee, burning its body from the inside. It uttered a choked scream of pain that fell silent halfway through, then its body exploded, sending chunks of meat everywhere and covering much of the area in thick black sludge.

"Ew," Thunder said as he landed where the nuckelavee was.

He picked up the staff and with one flick of it, managed to pull what was left of the nuckelavee into a raging whirlwind. With a second flick, he sent the whirlwind off into the woods in the direction of a nearby river. Thunder jogged over to the tree where Tala and Wolf were. During the fight, Tala had managed to successfully remove the spear with very minimal bleeding and pain, but there was still a gaping hole in his shoulder. She was in the process of ripping apart his shirt to try and staunch what she couldn't with magic.

"Where's River? He might be able to close it," Thunder asked, looking around.

"He's... He's dead," Tala replied, sounding like she was on the brink of tears.

The news caught Thunder by surprise, causing him to take a second to compose himself.

"Where's Forest then?" Thunder asked calmly.

Tala pointed to the uprooted tree on the other side of the clearing.

"Is he—?" Thunder began.

"I don't know, I haven't had a chance to check. Please, Dad, we can't let them die!" Tala burst into tears, frantically tying scraps of cloth around Wolf's body.

Wolf gritted his teeth and smiled uneasily at Thunder before tilting his head towards the tree that Forest was on. Thunder nodded and jogged over to it. Forest's body was completely mangled, with his limbs bent at awkward angles and his chest visibly deformed. Thunder knelt down and leaned close to Forest's mouth. He could feel air moving in and out of Forest's mouth, though it was faint. He offered a quiet thanks to the gods as he straightened back up.

Damn, he thought, *I really wish I knew enough about healing magic to try and help.*

The most he could do was set a couple bones and heal some bruises, but this... No, this was far beyond his understanding of magic. He was certain that it was only through the grace of some god somewhere that Forest was even still alive, for however long he might still be. Thunder jogged back over to Tala as she was just finishing her makeshift bandages on Wolf.

"Is... Is he...?" She asked, gasping slightly from the tears.

"No. He's still alive, but I don't know for how much longer," Thunder replied.

"Here, watch Wolf," Tala ordered, wiping her face.

"What are you gonna do?" Thunder replied, handing her the staff.

"I can't mend the bones, but I can at least set them so that they aren't harder to mend when the healers get here," Tala said, walking over to Forest's resting spot.

Though she acted like she was up for the task, Thunder knew it was just that. Thunder had broken more than his fair share of bones in his youth, both his and other people's, and he knew that setting the bone was excruciating. Tala reached Forest and leaned down, and though he couldn't see exactly what she was doing, Thunder could hear Forest cry out in pain. Flinching slightly, Thunder turned to Wolf.

"How are you doing?" he asked.

Wolf replied by raising his left hand and wagging it back and forth. *So so.*

"This is a stupid question, but can you tell me what happened here?"

Wolf shook his head and gestured to his bandages.

"Thought so. What about you, Horse?" Thunder asked, his voice taking on a much more serious octave.

Fear shot through Horse like an icy blade down the spine. He tried to open his mouth but only made a choking noise. Thunder stepped in front of the tree and pulled the young man out by the collar of his shirt. Thunder stood both head and shoulders over Horse, who looked even smaller as he cowered away.

"There... There was nothing I could do to help," Horse whispered.

"Really? Because I seem to think there are a lot of things you could've done," Thunder answered.

"It... It was too fast. I couldn't react in time," Horse muttered.

"So, you shit your pants and run? While my *daughter* was out here fighting for her life, the lives of all of you, *and* our village?" Thunder demanded.

Horse lowered his head and didn't answer.

"Answer. Me," Thunder enunciated each syllable with a venom.

"I was scared," Horse refused to look up at Thunder as he spoke.

"And you think they weren't?"

Before he could respond, the sound of pounding footsteps snapped Thunder back to attention. A squad of ten people led by Thunder's brother-in-law, Wounded Hawk, entered the clearing in a full sprint. The group of healers was an even mix of men and women, who immediately split into pairs and began to see to the wounded.

Two of them gathered what was left of River, another team went to Thunder, a third to Wolf, the fourth to Forest, and the final team to Tala. Hawk began to make his way over to Horse, but was stopped by Thunder.

"No, he took the coward's way out," Thunder said.

Hawk looked to Thunder, then to the destruction surrounding them, then spat at Horse's feet.

"Then the least he can do is help with the wounded," Hawk said, drawing Horse's eyes.

"No. He'll carry River back to the village," Thunder ordered.

"Sounds like a fitting punishment," Hawk replied.

"Not yet, it isn't." Thunder pointed over to Tala.

She stood a foot away from Forest and was completely dazed as the two healers checked her body for injuries, only occasionally wincing when they touched a tender area. Thunder could see the hollow look in her eyes from where he was standing and could tell what was going through her head. Hawk watched as the healer lifted his niece's arm to show a long bruise underneath her forearm and grimaced.

"Sometimes I think you're not hard enough, but this time..." He dropped his voice to just above a whisper, "This time, I think you need to make his life unbearable."

Hawk walked over to the healers who were working on Forest, but not before stopping to check on Tala.

"Are you okay, sweetie?" he asked.

She didn't speak, merely jerking her head in a nodding motion.

"A few broken bones, but none that need immediate attention. She should be okay for the return trip," one of the healers answered.

Hawk nodded and headed to speak with Forest's healers.

"Is he going to make it?" Hawk asked.

"Honestly, if it wasn't for Tala setting his bones, no. The pain of it was enough to spike his adrenaline and keep him alive long enough for us to seal any internal damage. It's still kinda rough though," one healer said, touching a small caduceus to Forest's head.

Tala perked her head up.

"He'll... He'll make it?" she asked.

"It's more likely than it would be if you hadn't set his bones for us," the healer replied.

Tears welled in Tala's eyes as she forced a smile, but it immediately vanished when the healers who were gathering River's remains came over to report they were finished.

"I believe Forest is in stable enough condition to move," one of his healers added.

"What about Wolf?" Hawk called across the clearing.

"With the stanched bleeding, it wasn't too difficult to close the bulk of the wounds, but we still have a long way to go," one healer called back.

"Let's get them on the move, it'll be less of a risk if they're back at the village," Hawk ordered.

The healers and their charges regrouped in the center of the clearing, by the ward stone. Forest was being carried over the shoulders of one healer, Wolf was being supported by one, and Hawk handed the bag with the remains of River to Horse, taking great pleasure in the boy's discomfort. The group headed back into the woods, but Hawk turned to see Thunder standing beside Tala next to the ward stone. Seeing him look, Thunder raised a hand and waved. Taking the hint, Hawk turned around and joined his squad.

Thunder leaned against the broken ward stone as Tala stared blankly at it. It was a few minutes before Thunder broke the silence.

"Beating yourself up about it won't change what happened," he said.

Tala didn't say anything in response, so he continued, "The worst part about being a leader are the people you lose. You start with a squad of five, and because of one small mistake, you barely escape with your own life, let alone one of your teammates. It eats away at you, telling you if you had done something different, been a little faster, a little stronger, or chosen another path, then maybe things would be different. What if you'd gone to the ward stone to the east? Would you have missed the nuckelavee here? Would River still be alive? That's what you're thinking, right?"

Tala jerked her head up in response, her eyes not leaving the ground.

"You'll spend so much time thinking about what went wrong that you'll forget to see what went right. River's death is a tragedy, that's true. He was a great man and will be missed by everyone, but you also managed to save the lives of Wolf and Forest single-handedly," Thunder explained.

"If I hadn't dropped my staff..." Tala whispered.

"But you did, Tala. It was written in the stars that this would happen. Fate played out how it was written to, and there's no use in beating yourself up about it," Thunder said, placing a hand on her shoulder.

Tala looked up at him with tears in her eyes.

"What am I supposed to do, just say, 'Oh well, sucks to be you' and move on? He died in front of me! I saw the look of pain pass over his face as the rocks... Gods, the rocks ripped him apart like nothing!" She yelled through the tears.

"You take every loss in life, and you learn from it. Mourn the fallen, remember their lives, and learn from their deaths so that in the future, you don't make the same mistake twice," Thunder explained.

He pulled her into a hug as she sobbed against his chest. They stayed like that for a minute until Tala finally calmed down enough to speak.

"We should... fix the ward..." She hiccupped.

"Of course," Thunder replied.

He took her staff, and with a flick of his wrist, all of the pieces of the ward stone flew back together and melded into each other again.

"Do you wanna do the honors?" he asked, handing her staff back.

She took the staff and touched the ward stone with it.

"Hear me, oh great goddesses of magic, protect our village from those that would seek its destruction, from beasts from the deepest pits of Tartarus itself, and from the creatures that fear the Great Scriptures of the Buddha himself. We, your humble servants of the Wind Swept Village, ask this in the name of Isis, Hecate, and Freyja," she prayed.

As she listed the names of the goddesses, she tapped three points of light into the ward stone, forming a triangle. The one at the top was bright yellow, the one to the right was a deep purple, and the one to the left was orange. A line of silver light traced the shape of the triangle, and the silver wall flashed into existence, before returning to being invisible.

"Who taught you that one?" Thunder asked when she finished.

"No one, it just came to me," Tala replied.

"Huh, interesting," Thunder muttered.

He turned and began walking to the woods, with Tala not far behind him.

"Hey, Dad?"

"Hmm?"

"How many people have you lost?"

Thunder didn't reply immediately, choosing to take a long, slow inhale first. He blew the air out of his nose before replying, "The mistakes of a parent are there so that we know what to pass down to the next generation and what not to. It doesn't matter how many people I've lost. It only matters how many people I can stop you from losing."

Chapter 5

Gaius had been flying for a few hours and was starting to get hungry.

Damn, I should've grabbed something this morning. Now, I'll have to hunt down some food, clean it, cook it, this is gonna like... half the day at least.

Lowering himself to the ground, he landed in the middle of a dense forest.

Good thing I can fly. Sure would suck to get lost out here.

He started to trek in the same direction he had been going, slowly and quietly, so as not to scare off any potential prey. He spotted a couple of squirrels, but nothing too big to eat. As he walked, he began to think about the events from earlier this morning. Just who was that old woman? Some of the things she said were so strange that Gaius had difficulty wrapping his head around them. Beings higher than gods? Could she mean titans? No, that wasn't possible, after the Titanomachy, Zeus imprisoned them all. All except the select few that chose to join him that is. Still though, none of them would want to overthrow the gods. Themis was still heavily favored by all as a goddess of justice, and Prometheus hadn't been seen for centuries. The stories say that he traveled to Muspelheim and is living amongst the fire giants. He seriously doubted that either would have a motive against the gods.

Gaius didn't kid himself, though. Despite all of their propaganda otherwise, everyone knew the gods had enemies. The giants had started wars with damn near every pantheon, but despite their power and numbers, they seemed to lack a unified front. There were an innumerable number of demons, yokai, and monsters that all opposed the gods, but very few of them lacked the power to seriously wound a god. There was no way they were truly immortal, despite what they say. The gods aged, and there were even stories of certain gods dying. Gaius knew for a fact that the Egyptian gods could die, frequently died, but were always reincarnated in the womb of another member of their pantheon.

Must make birthdays a bitch, Gaius thought. *Would you tell Isis happy birthday mom, or happy birthday sister?*

He chuckled to himself before stopping to look around. There had to be a deer or something somewhere, yet he had not found one.

Maybe this is why I was never allowed to go hunting.

He exhaled a sigh of annoyance before closing his eyes. Focusing his mind, he released a rush of psychic energy in all directions around him. His awareness swept past snakes, squirrels, rabbits, and various insects, their locations revealed to him. It wasn't until he touched the mind of a large stag roughly two hundred yards to his left that he took notice.

Due to years of reconnaissance and battle, Gaius had no real difficulty holding a mental link at a range like that, so he burrowed into the creature's mind. Unsurprisingly, the creature thought like a regular animal. Its only thoughts were focused on the grass at its feet that it was chewing on. Searching the animal's mind, Gaius learned that it had a den with a small family, a doe and two fawns, to be specific. Memorizing the location of the den for future usage, he could find anything else of value in the animal's mind.

To me, Gaius' thought enforced itself on the creature.

There was a moment of intense fear and panic in the animal's mind, but Gaius quickly overrode it with his will. The stag's mind became empty, except for the compulsion to come to Gaius.

Gaius steered it to him until he could hear it coming through the woods, and opened his eyes to it standing before him. The stag's eyes were glazed over, completely empty of any thought or emotion. It stared at

Gaius as he calmly walked over and placed a hand on its fur. Gaius ran a hand down its majestic fur before pulling back and snapping his fingers.

The stag's neck twisted quickly as it let out a reflexive bleat that was silenced by the sound of twisting bones. The stag fell dead at Gaius' feet. He flicked his wrist, summoning a blade of psychic energy and set to work skinning, gutting, and cleaning it. As he worked, he thought about the first time he had ever learned he could override a creature's mind like that.

It had only been two weeks since Thunder took Gaius in. He had tried to be helpful but wasn't really good at anything. He kept accidentally pulling crops, instead of weeds. He wasn't able to sew. He couldn't fish, hunt, or cook.

In truth, his only useful qualities were his psionic abilities. It made things easier for him, yes, but they couldn't fill every gap in his skill set. They were sitting in the mead hall for Thunder's weekly tradition he called "Listening Day."

At the end of the week, he would set aside an entire day to hear the problems of the village and do his best to resolve them. On this day, the farmer, Grass Whisperer, was the only villager to arrive that day and told them of a grave issue that could threaten the village: mice had infested the grain house.

"You're right, this is a serious issue. Those mice could eat through our grain, or worse, infect it with their droppings and make the whole village sick," Thunder's answer was immediate, deliberate, and sincere.

Gaius was mildly confused but was surprised when Thunder asked him to join him. Thunder explained that he and Gaius had magic that could activate faster than a mouse could react, meaning they were the best suited for wiping out the infestation. They went with Grass to the grain house, and the three took up posts in the rafters of the house, watching silently, like cats waiting for their prey.

They waited for hours.

Gaius began so incredibly bored that his mind began to wander, quite literally. He expanded his consciousness outwards and scanned around the house. He wasn't trying to find anything, just looking for something to bide his time. His mind scraped by Thunder's, which he recognized by its high sense of duty and responsibility, and the mind of Grass, which was filled with a surprising joy and fulfillment. Curiosity sent him wandering closer to the ground when he felt something hiding under a bale of hay. Reaching over, he found a small mouse chewing on some hay.

Much eat. Lead out brood. Watch for giants. Its mind was so primal that it was like a blank sheet of paper to Gaius.

It was a simple creature and only driven by base desires. It had no real emotions, just contentment with itself and the fear of death. It didn't seem to notice Gaius' presence as it chewed on its hay, so he dug a little deeper into its mind.

The location of its small burrow and massive family were soon revealed to Gaius, and he extended his mind to it. It was a small, almost unnoticeable hole in the ground behind a barrel in the corner. Gaius reached into it, and found hundreds of consciousnesses in it.

Males, females, children and elderly all squirmed over each other in a mass of single-minded, animal instincts. Gaius recoiled in disgust momentarily, until an idea reached his mind. Paper was meant to be written on, right? So, why shouldn't he write over the minds of these rodent pests and have them leave and never return?

Grinning to himself, Gaius used the first mouse to test the limits of this newfound ability. He burrowed into the animal's mind. It resisted at first, but its simple little brain was no match for Gaius. He exerted control and soon the mouse's brain was his.

Gaius had opted to try and take direct control for the first phase of his experiment, and tried to move it like a puppet. The nervous system that controlled the mouse was a bit tricky to figure out, and after roughly two minutes, all he did was make it take a step forward, then fall over. Frustrated, Gaius pulled away from the mind to regain his bearings.

After a few seconds, he returned to probing the mouse and found that simply giving commands like a trainer to a dog was much simpler. He told the mouse to move forward, and it responded. It went backward, stood on its hind legs, grabbed some hay, and jumped. Gaius was delighted and pulled away from the mouse, relieved to find that its mind wasn't ultimately damaged by his presence.

Turning his attention to the burrow, Gaius plunged inside again and could feel the many hundreds of consciousnesses inside. He paused for a second to consider his actions. Going from one mouse to close to a thousand wasn't going to be an easy task.

What if something happened to him? What if he lost himself in the mice and couldn't get out? He pondered thoughts like that for a second, before ultimately deciding he was more curious than cautious and diving into the hole. With a surprising deal of effort in an equally surprisingly short period of time, Gaius learned how to fracture his consciousness and took control of every mouse in the burrow.

It was a bizarre sensation to occupy that many minds. There were so many different sensations, desires, and thoughts. Each mouse seemed to want something different. Most wanted food, but some wanted to breed, some wanted to dig, and others wanted some more immediate goals.

One mouse wanted another to stop stepping on its tail, one wanted to crawl out and get some fresh air, and another one desperately wanted to relieve itself. The barrage of sensations, from the feeling of all the mice rubbing against each other, to them all smelling the same dirt and droppings, to even them all seeing vague shapes in the darkness, started to completely overwhelm Gaius' mind.

When the blood started to drip from his nose, he originally thought it was just from a mouse and didn't worry about it. He decided it was time to see what all he'd be capable of with this ability.

Leave the burrow.

The resulting rumble of activity almost brought Gaius to his knees, and he was vaguely aware of someone talking around his body. The mice all proceeded out of their burrow and swarmed the corner. Once again, someone close to his body said something that he couldn't hear.

Out the door. Do not return.

The mice all marched forward like soldiers to a battlefield, even taking a second for Gaius to pick up the stray under the bale of hay. It seemed that getting closer to Gaius restored some of his mind because he heard Thunder shout and start casting a spell. Shaking his head, Gaius brought himself back to his body.

"No! Stop!" Gaius yelled.

Everything ceased movement at once, from the mice to Thunder himself. Thunder stared down at the mice before looking back to Gaius. No one spoke for a few seconds.

"Gaius... What's going on?" Thunder asked.

Gaius stared down in genuine shock and amazement before jumping from the rafters and landing in front of the mice.

"I'm controlling them, I guess," Gaius replied.

"All of them?" Grass asked.

"Yeah, watch this," Gaius said, before issuing a command for the mice to all stand.

The action was followed seamlessly, and Gaius laughed in amusement.

"Okay... How exactly are you controlling them?" Thunder asked, a nervous edge to his voice.

Gaius proceeded to explain the last few minutes to them, and they listened in horrified intrigue.

"So, you're basically erasing their minds and using them as puppets?" Grass asked.

"What? No. Their minds are fine, watch," Gaius said, picking up a nearby mouse.

After spending a couple of seconds finding its consciousness in the mass, Gaius released control of it, and it began to spin around in his palm, sniffing it before running up his arm.

"See? It's fine. Back to normal with no— OW!" Gaius yelped as the mouse bit him on the thumb.

Out of reflex, Gaius clenched the mouse, and a sudden flash of psychic energy enveloped it. The mouse seemed to go limp in his hand as a result.

"Did you kill it?" Thunder asked, jumping down beside him.

"What? No, it's still alive. I can feel it breathing," Gaius answered, opening his palm.

Grass leapt down to investigate, and the three could very well see that the mouse was in fact still breathing, and its heart was still beating.

"What did you do to it?" Grass asked.

"I... I don't know." Gaius whispered.

He reached out to touch its mind and found nothing. There were no thoughts, conscious or primal, no emotions, desires, drives or anything. It was completely blank beyond what ran automatically for survival. It kept the lungs breathing and the heart pumping, but that was it. Gaius pulled back in shock and stood for a second before speaking.

"There's nothing there," he said.

Thunder and Grass looked at each other before inspecting the mouse.

"What do you mean?" Thunder asked, poking the mouse with a finger.

Gaius explained that the mind of the mouse was completely barren, and they said nothing for a few seconds. Gaius doesn't fully remember what happened next, but he remembered his body giving out and Grass and Thunder trying to catch him. He woke up later that day in the healer's hut with Tala and Thunder at his side.

After Tala exchanged her pleasantries with him being awake, she left him and Thunder alone. Thunder stared out the window for a minute before he said anything.

"Gaius, that thing you did with the mice, you can never do it again," Thunder said.

"What? Why?" Gaius asked, drowsily.

"The mind of a creature is a sacred thing. It's where we store the memories, thoughts and emotions that make us who we are. The ability to take control of something's mind, let alone the ability to destroy it, is... Well, it's just not right. Taking away a being's bodily autonomy and forcing them to do what you want them to do is the way of monsters and tyrants, not heroes. Despite that, being able to destroy something's mind is worse. Erasing a creature's very being is unheard of, but it's worse than being used like a puppet. To lose yourself, your purpose, that's no existence worth living in, even if it wouldn't be for long. Do you understand?" Thunder explained.

Gaius nodded, the sudden motion sending an unbearable scream of agony through his mind. He laid there still for a while after Thunder left and began to scan through his body for any pain. Not feeling anything made him realize that over-extending his powers like that could easily damage his brain and leave him seriously injured. He made a mental note of that fact and resolved to work his powers like a muscle until they were strong enough to be used more consistently. He tried to psychically grab the glass of water on his stand and was almost crippled by the pain.

Tomorrow, he thought, *I'll start working on that tomorrow.*

Though he would never admit it to Thunder, he spent the next few years learning how to hone those abilities to a mirror shine. After all, whether it was the right thing to do or not, it was always handy to be able to erase something's entire mind, or even just parts of it, at will.

The sound of a growl brought Gaius out of his thoughts. Taking a second to look around, he saw a wolf standing near his little campsite, eyeing the meat and pile of viscera. Gaius reached out with his mind and touched the wolf's psyche. It was hungry, but it wouldn't attack if it wasn't provoked.

You can have the viscera and organs, but stay away from the meat, Gaius thought to it.

The wolf cocked its head in surprise, staring at Gaius for a second. It seemed to come to a decision since it walked around the fire and snapped up a whole mouthful of the pile of viscera and began to eat. When it was finished, it wagged its tail and offered a short bark as thanks. Gaius gave a quick two finger salute as an acknowledgment, and the wolf trekked back into the forest. Psychically checking the meat, Gaius laid back and watched the clouds roll overhead.

I wonder what Tala's doing right now, he thought, *probably planning out every detail of our big day.* He chuckled to himself. *Nah, that's all too girly for her. Thunder's definitely doing it though.*

Once the meat was ready, he ate a decent lunch, storing the rest in his knapsack for later, and flew into the sky again, resuming his quest towards Olympus.

Chapter 6

The rest of Gaius' week continued in a similar manner, he flew until he got hungry, ate, flew until night, then slept. After mastering flight, he practiced it so much that it barely strained his powers anymore. Around noon on the seventh day after leaving the village, he landed in the large city roughly ten miles from the base of Olympus. Thunder had told him about this city a few years ago.

Apparently, it was a hotspot for tourism, with many people wanting to speak to the oracles, or try and have an audience with the gods, or even get the chance to have an affair with one of the gods. Gaius didn't know much about history, but he was aware that the Olympians were the primary reason for the existence of the Heracles Accords, though it was widely speculated that they didn't follow them.

Gaius had landed outside the city and decided to walk in through the main road to draw as little attention as possible. From the outside, the city looked like a massive walled fortress with a guard checkpoint standing outside of the gate. Gaius tried to slip by unnoticed, but was caught by a guard who placed a hand on his shoulder. He was an older man with a gray beard and white hair wearing some leather armor with a spear in one hand, a scimitar on his right hip, and a shield on his back.

"Woah, there, sonny. I can't let you in that easily. Gotta tell me your name, your business here, and where you come from first," the old man said politely.

Gaius had predicted this would happen, and so he composed a fake story in his head a few days prior.

"Oh, yeah. Sorry about that. My name's Jason Valorsson, I was sent here by my father to try and see if there was a spot in the city where we might be able to open up a store. We're wandering nomads who have gotten tired of fending off monsters and are looking to set up a store in a good town." Gaius recited his story with ease, hoping its fluidity would give credit to the story.

The guard stared at him for a second.

"What kind of goods do you sell?" he asked.

"Pottery, mostly, but my mother knows her way around a sewing wheel if she gets the right fabric," Gaius replied.

The guard seemed to be brightened by this.

"Ah, wonderful. I recommend taking a stroll through the central district, there might be a few open spots for some stalls down there," he said with a smile.

He clapped Gaius on the back and let him walk through.

Nice fellow, shame I had to lie to him, Gaius thought to himself.

Entering the city gates, he was dumbstruck by everything around him. Hundreds of people walked the streets talking, eating food that smelled delicious, and wearing some of the finest attire he had ever seen. Many of the buildings were stone and stood a couple stories high, and the city seemed to stretch for miles in either direction. He walked through the city, following signs for inns and other amenities and soon found himself at the door to a massive four-storied inn called 'The Sleepin' Inn.' He stood outside for a second, shaking his head at the stupid pun name, before heading inside.

The inside had a small lobby area with a set of stairs leading to the higher floors and a balcony on each level. There was a small desk by the stairs with a bored-looking young woman reading a book. As Gaius approached, she glanced up and immediately returned to the book.

"Welcome to The Sleepin' Inn, the only room you'll wanna be sleepin' in. How can I assist you today?" her voice sounded even more bored than her eyes.

“Um... Hi. I was wondering if I could get a room?” Gaius asked.

“How long would your stay be?” she asked.

“No more than two, maybe three days.”

“Floor preference?”

“Any one is fine.”

“How many people are with you?”

“Just myself.”

“A standard, one person room on the first floor would cost you three hundred and forty-seven gold for a three-day stay.”

“What the shit?”

The way she spoke so bored and nonchalantly completely surprised Gaius, but not nearly as much as the price for the room.

I don’t think I brought enough gold, Gaius thought.

Reluctantly, he forked over a large portion of the money he had brought with him for this trip. It had taken him months to earn all the money he brought, and it physically pained his chest to watch the woman causally count it out like it meant nothing. After a few seconds, she opened a drawer with a key and deposited the gold, while grabbing a key from inside it.

“First floor, eastern hallway, last room on the right,” she said, pointing at the stairs.

Gaius took the key and followed her directions, finding himself in a small room with one bed and a wardrobe against the wall. There was a window above the bed that seemed to face another building outside. Exhausted from his week of straight traveling, he laid down on the bed and fell into a quiet nap.

After a few hours, he awoke to see the shadow of the sun setting and could hear music outside the inn. He sat up and looked out the window, but all he could see was a small alley between the inn and the building behind it. He could hear a great deal of music and laughter, though, and this piqued his curiosity.

I had planned to... Well, plan while I stay here. I doubt a night on the town would hurt, though.

Gaius got up and headed downstairs, finding the lobby of the inn completely empty. He headed to the door and headed outside. Outside the inn was a sight that completely took his breath away. The whole city was lit up with torches, lanterns, and floating spheres of light. The town center was filled with people dancing as a band played beautifully upbeat music on a stage.

Even more people wandered around drinking, laughing, and seeming to be having a jolly old time. Vendors sold food that sizzled and tankards of various kinds of alcohol, magicians performed street magic for gold, guards marched the streets, pulling away anyone who started a fight or got too handsy with someone else. He was surprised, even on the biggest nights of the year for Wind Swept Village, there were never enough people to cause this much of a ruckus.

He looked around and saw a nearby vendor selling sizzling meat and peppers on a stick, and the sight made his mouth water. He made his way through the crowd and found himself in front of the vendor.

"Well hello, stranger. I've got these meat sticks here in both spicy and sweet, as well as some mead made from my own personal beehives. What can I get you?" the vendor asked with a wide smile.

"How much for a spicy one?" Gaius asked.

"Five gold." The vendor replied, grabbing a stick.

As Gaius fished through his pockets for the gold, the man stabbed the meat and peppers onto the stick and handed it over. Gaius had only a hundred gold left, so he'd have to be careful with his spending, but the food looked so good he couldn't help himself. After the exchange, he started to walk away before stopping. An icy chill ran up his spine as he looked behind him, scanning the crowd. No one seemed to be paying him any mind, but for some reason, he felt his eyes drawn to a small alley between two stores. He couldn't see anything, but he felt compelled to let his eyes linger for a minute. Then, just as suddenly as it had started, the feeling vanished.

Man, this week has been weird. First the dream, then that old woman, and now this. Maybe those beings the old crone were talking about are watching me.

The thought wasn't a pleasant one, so Gaius decided not to try and think about it. After all, no one seemed to have any real worries tonight. Gaius didn't know what the occasion was, but frankly, he didn't care. The music, smells, and sounds of people laughing and enjoying themselves all filled him with an energy he had never felt before.

As he walked, he found himself smiling, exchanging pleasantries with random strangers, and enjoying himself.

He finished off his snack in a few minutes and was starting to get hungry again. He arrived at another vendor who was selling plates of rice covered with some kind of spicy sauce. He approached the table and was greeted with a smile from the vendor, a young woman with brown skin wearing a blue dress with her black hair pulled into a braid.

"Hello, how can I help you?" she asked, with a slight accent that Gaius couldn't place.

"Hi. I was wondering how much for a plate of your..." he began, trailing off as he didn't know what the dish was.

"Curry?" she supplied.

"Yes, that. How much for a plate?" Gaius asked.

"Twenty-five gold." She replied, grabbing a plate.

Gaius was about to stop her when he realized something. He shouldn't be paying for anything here. He was about to become a god, and people should pay tribute to their gods. The idea dug into his mind with such viciousness that it caught him off guard.

Gaius wasn't entirely sure where it came from as he had never stolen anything. Thunder taught him that people should pay their way forward, because everyone's work was valuable. This thought seemed to be completely against his morals, and yet... It didn't sound too bad, either. Gaius found the thought intoxicating and didn't hesitate to jump at it.

Without a second thought, he dove into the young woman's mind and implanted a memory of her giving the curry to him in exchange for money. She smiled, completely oblivious, as he thanked her, took the curry and walked away.

After finding a spot to sit down, Gaius noticed his hands were shaking. He wasn't nervous though, rather he was bursting at the seams from the excitement for what he did. The feeling gripped at his psyche to the point where he became drunk with it. If it felt this good to use his powers to take food, why didn't he use it to get more?

A couple had started to walk past while Gaius ate his curry, and he decided that he wanted their money. Burrowing into their minds, he placed that one single command. The man and woman turned to him with glazed expressions and handed over forty gold apiece, before heading back on their way like nothing happened.

The night went on like that for a while, with Gaius utilizing his powers to have people give him free drinks, free food, and money from anyone who looked like they had more than enough. Gaius eventually grew both tired and bored, so he decided to return to his room.

After the events of the evening, however, he felt it might be better if he went back inside the inn more discreetly than simply through the front door. He wasn't sure if anyone had seen his actions tonight, so he decided it would be better if he took some precautions. Walking around to the back alley where his room was, he prepared to fly up to his window when he heard a noise.

From behind some boxes, a group of four individuals holding knives emerged and crept up to him. One of them, a tall young man with brown hair wearing a cloth mask covering most of his face, stepped forward.

"All right, let's make this real easy. You give us your money, and we won't gut you like a fish. Simple enough?" he said, pointing his knife at Gaius.

At first, Gaius thought about sending them flying out into the street and getting back in his room before they could recover, but another thought hit him. These guys could easily hurt someone that wasn't him. He had a perfect chance to stop that.

With a quick flick of his hand, the arms of all four people became encased in blue light. They panicked and began to shout, so Gaius flicked his wrist with two fingers extended and slammed their jaws shut. He saw tears from the leader as his mouth oozed blood, and Gaius assumed he had just severed or at least damaged his tongue by biting it.

Gaius quickly clenched his fist, and the alley became filled with muffled screams and the sounds of breaking bones. He made sure to snap every bone in their arms and hands in an attempt to leave them permanently damaged. After running a quick scan through their nerves to verify he had succeeded, Gaius forcefully pushed a hand at them, sending a gust of psychic energy that sent them flying back deeper into the alley.

As they groaned and sobbed, Gaius quickly became invisible to avoid further detection and flew up to his window to enter his room.

Once back inside, he closed the window, laid down and went to sleep. He had a big day tomorrow, and he was going to need all the strength he could muster.

Chapter 7

The last week was rough for Tala. Many people held her as a hero, but she couldn't see herself that way. She still felt she had failed Forest, Wolf, and especially River. Her own recovery didn't take too long, so she spent most of her time at the hospital, trying her best to help her uncle and the other healers bring the two back from the brink of fading.

Though she wasn't a medic, she was more than willing to lend the doctors her staff, or her flow of magic to help close wounds or mend bones. The doctors told her that it helped exponentially speed up recovery. By the second day, the holes in both Wolf's torso and shoulder were healed, and by the third he was up walking.

Forest's recovery took some more time. A few times, the healers had to re-break bones that had healed in the wrong positions. Though they tried to keep it quiet, Tala heard them talking about the lasting damage he would suffer. They were certain he'd never walk without a cane again, and might suffer some serious pains from cold and rainy weather. The constant reforming of his left arm seemed to have damaged his nerves and made his left hand almost unusable. Luckily, his spine would suffer no serious damage right now, but they weren't sure about it in the future.

The only person Tala couldn't care less about was Horse. He had tried to speak to her, but she ignored him. The only time she paid him any mind was when she knew her father had decided on his verdict for Horse. Horse was to spend the next three summers collecting manure from Grass Whisperer's cows, and using it to fertilize the three-acre farm. During winter, it would be his personal responsibility to keep all paths in the village free of snow and ice without the use of magic. He had begged Tala to convince Thunder to reconsider his verdict, and Tala punched him in the face with enough force to knock him to the ground.

"You were too scared of getting your hands dirty to help, maybe next time you'll be used to it," she had told him.

The wake for River was set for the end of the week, and the whole village was expected to attend—even Horse. As his partner, Forest was supposed to give the sermon, but Tala wasn't sure if he'd be able to, given the state of his legs. Still, he had insisted. Tala had spent much of the week worrying herself sick about it.

When the day came, Thunder told her that Forest had specifically asked for her not to come to the hospital, but he did want her at the wake. She had agreed, and now sat quietly in the first row, between Wolf and her Father.

As was tradition, the wake was to be held in the town hall, which had required some prep work of its own. They had pushed the tables against the walls, and turned the long benches into pews for sitting. Luckily, the town didn't have many people, so they could still fit everyone into the hall. The first row was to be reserved for the family of the deceased, as well as the chief himself, who would supply a few words after the family had spoken.

Sadly, however, River had lost his parents the winter before to a sickness, leaving the main row empty, save for Tala, Thunder, and Wolf. Wolf had asked if he could speak as well, which broke tradition, but Thunder decided to allow it since Wolf was the closest thing to a brother that River had.

After the town had fully filed in and had taken their seats, Thunder stood up and walked to the podium that had been set up. He raised his hand to quiet everyone, and pressed his hands together in a prayer motion.

Everyone in the village did the same, and they sat quiet, offering silent prayers to the gods of the underworld. After a minute, Thunder raised his head and stepped off stage, his footsteps echoing as he walked down.

When he took his seat, the doors to the hall opened, and Forest limped in, flanked by a pair of doctors. He walked with a cane and seemed to have trouble fully balancing, often swaying and being caught by one of the doctors. Very slowly and carefully, the group approached the podium. The doctors took a seat in the first row after Thunder offered them a nod of approval, leaving Forest to limp the last few feet by himself.

It took him a couple of seconds longer than it would for others, but he made it around the podium. He stood there for a minute, his face red and covered in sweat from the effort of being on his feet again so soon. It took him a few seconds to catch his breath and begin his eulogy.

"River would often tell me that he wondered how I would survive without him. After all, I'm accident-prone and seemingly cursed with bad luck. I would often respond that I'd probably never find out, because my bad luck would take me first." He offered a light chuckle before continuing, "I guess I was wrong though. This past week has been rough with my constant and seemingly never-ending stay in the hospital, but not having River has made it worse. I think everyone can attest to that. I don't have to tell you how great of a man River was. He helped everyone in town in any way he could. He was a man of many talents, from farming and hunting to pottery and storytelling. Whenever someone had a hard day, he offered a shoulder and a smile. I wish I had that now. Now that he's gone, all I have are the memories. If there's one memory I want everyone to remember, it's this: River always thought the future would be bright, even in the worst times."

Forest wiped his eyes and limped away from the podium before sitting down beside Thunder. Once he sat down, Wolf's spectral wolf appeared on stage.

"I don't truly know what to say. I'm still in shock that he's gone, it all just happened so fast. Truth be told, River was more of a brother than a friend. His family took me in and raised me after my father died while hunting, and since then, he and I were inseparable. It truly doesn't feel real, losing someone like that. May he rest in peace, and may we see him again in Valhalla," Wolf said.

His wolf disappeared in a gust of wind, and Thunder got back up and walked to the podium.

"River will be missed but not forgotten. He helped all of us and was a core member of our community. Moving forward, I only ask that we honor his memory and strive to be people nearly as good as him," Thunder spoke the words with solemnness in his voice.

He gave a longer speech after that, but Tala had stopped listening and was focusing on the broken man two chairs over from her. Forest looked over and smiled. He reached over and placed a hand on her shoulder, squeezing it gently.

"Don't blame yourself. It's not your fault," he whispered.

"If I—," she began.

"No," he cut her off softly, but firmly. "It's not your fault. We didn't know it would do something like that. None of us could've prepared for it. The last thing River would want you to do is beat yourself up over something you couldn't control."

She felt a hand on her other shoulder and looked over to see Wolf nodding in agreement. Tala lowered her head and took a deep breath before letting out a long, low sigh.

"I'll try. That's all I can do," she replied.

"That's all we ask," Forest's smile put some of her worries to rest. Tala sat quietly as Thunder finished his speech. The rest of the day was a somber blur to Tala, she ate during the feast, sang the songs around the bonfire, but she felt so disconnected from everything. It felt like she moved from place to place by blinking.

After the bonfire, Tala went to her room to lay down. She wasn't tired, but the last few days had worn her down both mentally and physically, and she was genuinely exhausted. She got out of her clothes, put on her nightgown, blew out her lantern and sat on her bed, staring at the shadows on the wall. She reached up and touched the necklace around her neck.

If Gaius had been here...

She laid down and twirled the necklace in her fingers. Shadows danced on the ceiling and Tala's eyes grew heavy. Before she realized it, she had fallen asleep.

Chapter 8

Tala woke up in the morning to the sun shining through her window. She didn't know what time it was, but it was the first time this week she had slept past dawn. She felt refreshed like an incredible weight was off her shoulders. She got dressed in her deerskin pants and gray cotton shirt. Grabbing her staff, she headed downstairs and entered the kitchen. She hadn't expected to see Thunder making breakfast already.

"Morning, Tala. Are you feeling any better?" he asked.

Tala surveyed the scene before her. The kitchen wasn't large, with a counter on one side and an ice box on one side. Next to it was a small furnace, a fireplace set into the far wall with a cauldron hanging above it. Next to the entry wall was a small nook carved into it, with a bench going around a table. The counter was covered with various broken egg shells, burnt pieces of bread, and random pieces of meat in various stages of cooking, from raw to 'why is that one on fire?'

"Um... Dad? I thought we agreed that I would do the cooking while Gaius was gone," Tala said, scratching her head.

"Well, yeah, but you had such a rough week that I thought I would surprise you with an omelet," Thunder replied, flipping a pan with something yellow inside. "Or... Scrambled eggs. I think this is now scrambled eggs."

Tala sighed and ran a hand through her hair.

"Ya know what? Scrambled eggs sound lovely. Thanks, Dad," Tala said, running a hand through her hair.

Thunder replied with a smile, which quickly turned into shock as the pan caught fire. Tala pursed her lips and sighed. With a wave of her staff, she conjured a small storm cloud over the pan that quickly rained out the fire.

"So... you think that a fruit breakfast sounds lovely too?" Thunder asked.

"Already on it," Tala replied, grabbing an apple from the ice box.

She tossed it to Thunder, who caught it and took a seat in the nook. Tala did the same, sitting across from him.

"Any plans for today?" she asked.

"Not much, really. I've got a few small things around the village. Grass wants to talk about the harvest, then just monitor the construction of the wall," Thunder replied.

"Need any help?" Tala asked.

"Not today, just relax and take it easy. Tomorrow, we can start some bigger projects," Thunder said.

They sat in silence for a few minutes.

"Can I ask you something?" Tala asked.

Thunder nodded, unable to speak through a mouth full of apple.

"What really happened to Mom?"

If he was surprised by her question, Thunder didn't show it. If anything, he most likely expected it. Taking a second to finish his bite, Thunder set down the apple, clasped his hands and gave her the stern, flat face she had seen him use for business negotiations.

"Are you sure you want to know?" he asked.

Tala steadied her face and mind as best she could, bracing herself for what was coming. She nodded in response, trying to suppress her rising emotions.

"The dragon isn't what killed your mother. When she hit that tree, it broke her right arm and several ribs on that side. She got back to her feet and went running to save Gaius, when his power... exploded," Thunder explained.

"What?"

"I think the heightened stress and seeing the dragon strike your mother caused Gaius' psychic abilities to violently release beyond his control. He completely shredded the dragon, but at the same time, Wind took a hit from the blast as well."

Tala sat silent for a few seconds, processing the information. When she didn't say anything, Thunder continued, "We found her completely mangled. Several bones were broken, with many puncturing organs, her skin was covered in bruises and lacerations, and she was barely breathing."

Again, Tala said nothing. Thunder decided to give her a chance to process the information, so he sat silently. For several seconds, the only noise came from Thunder spinning his apple on the table.

"Why didn't you tell me back then?" she asked.

"I didn't want you to blame Gaius. At that time, we still knew little to nothing about him, and the worst thing we could've done was punish him for something that wasn't his fault. I've seen how dangerous untrained and powerful magic is in the hands of a child. The accident wasn't his fault, and he already felt guilty about it. Putting more blame on him might have driven him away," Thunder explained.

Tala said nothing in response, but Thunder could see that she was considering his words. After a minute of silence, Thunder decided to ask a question, "Are you upset that I kept the truth from you?"

Tala shook her head.

"I think... I think you're right. I wouldn't have been ready to hear it back then," Tala replied.

Thunder finished his apple and got to his feet. He walked around the table and ruffled Tala's hair.

"Your mother would be proud of who you've become. Both of you," Thunder said softly.

Tala smiled in response, before getting up herself. The two tossed their apple cores into the small basket they used for scraps, and headed back to the main room of their little house.

“So, now that you’re free of any duties and responsibilities today, what’s your plan?” Thunder asked.

“I don’t know yet, maybe I’ll catch up on some reading or go practice magic now that my staff won’t detonate in my hands. I’ll probably just go for a walk around town though,” Tala replied.

Thunder nodded in response before heading out to the main mead hall, leaving Tala alone. She ate another apple, and set to work cleaning up the kitchen. After extinguishing some small burning pieces of meat, and gathering up all the trash, she quickly washed the pans and headed out herself.

The mead hall was pretty quiet this early in the morning, the only occupants being herself, her father and Grass Whisperer, who were locked in an important discussion about the upcoming harvest in three months. The two didn’t pay her any mind as she started past, but she stopped when Thunder mentioned trade with the southern Village of Three Rivers no longer being possible.

“The nuckelavee decimated the entire village. Many people died, and it could take years to rebuild their numbers. I doubt they’ll make it through the winter. We need a decent harvest this year, or we run the risk of losing a large number of our elderly and children,” Thunder explained.

“Trust me, I understand the predicament, but even with Horse’s help, I can only do so much. If I taught him the spells to hasten the growth of the crops, it could take weeks. Weeks we don’t have right now,” Grass replied, tapping his finger on the table.

“Why not just focus down a section?” Thunder asked.

"It could run the risk of the fields needing even more work next year to be viable. Starting from scratch is rough, that's why each year I have to tend to everything," Grass replied, sitting back in his chair.

"Damn, that accursed beast. Trade with Three Rivers was all we had after Falling Star was wiped out. There's gotta be something we can do," Thunder grumbled, resting his chin on his hand.

"How many people survived at Three Rivers?" Tala asked.

Thunder and Grass looked at her.

"Roughly sixty, if I remember right, twenty men and thirty women ranging from your age to in their sixties, and ten children, at least three of which have lost their parents. Why?" Thunder answered.

"Since they might not have a chance at surviving winter otherwise, see if they'd come with us. You can have the men help finish the wall so we can have it ready for winter, teach whoever can use magic different spells for different crops, and we can hurry and start stockpiling for winter," Tala explained, taking a seat at the table.

"We'd have more mouths to feed but also more help to do it," Grass said with a shrug.

"Sixty new people would be a lot. We don't have the housing or the bedding for it," Thunder said, shifting hands to look at his daughter.

"They can stay at the mead hall for winter, and come spring, we can start working on expanding the village to make more houses. Maybe we could add a second story to some homes, and let one family live on each floor," Tala explained.

"Too many people crammed together that long could cause sickness to spread," Thunder replied.

"Not with adequate healthcare from Uncle and the doctors," Tala retorted.

"Why are you so sure this could work?" Grass asked.

"Mother used to teach me to always have faith in something. Today, that faith is in the belief that we can save both our village and the lives of people who don't deserve to die because of some monster," Tala replied.

It was quiet for a minute as Thunder mulled over the choice before him. On one hand, it was a significant risk. One small misstep could lead the village to starvation or, worse, another epidemic. On the other hand, more people meant more hands to do the work.

With the upcoming harvest in three months, winter wouldn't be far behind. Getting the wall finished in time could mean the difference between life and death in the event of another blizzard. More hands on the farm meant more magic users could help grow and stockpile for winter.

Usually, new people didn't arrive in such a large number; a baby born here or there or a stranger stumbling into town half dead and needing to be nursed back was one thing, this... This was a whole different animal. One that Thunder had never encountered in his tenure as chief. It was a tough decision, but he followed his mind over his gut this time.

"This is a huge gamble, but it would have a much bigger payoff in the future. Let's saddle up a couple hunters, get a couple wagons and get down to Three Rivers. The sooner we get there, the more time we have to get everyone settled and start the long prep work for winter," Thunder said, getting up.

"I'll start getting the farm ready for the extra hands," Grass replied, also rising to his feet.

Tala started to head back outside, when Thunder stopped her.

"Where do you think you're going?" he asked firmly but without any malice.

"I thought I had the day off," Tala replied.

"You did, but this was your idea. Now, you'll be joining me and our team. This will give you a chance to learn to be a leader, and besides, these people will most likely be scared and unwilling to leave their homes. It'll do them good to meet the hero who held back the nuckelavee, give them a sense of security when they'll need it most," Thunder explained.

The words hung in the air around Tala with more weight than Yggdrasil itself. She knew that being a leader was a difficult task, and she thought she was ready for it, but the thought of trying to inspire a whole group of people to leave their homes and come to a place that might not even guarantee their safety was something she hadn't been ready for.

A quick thought of running away flashed through her mind, but she couldn't bring herself to act on it. She knew deep down she wasn't ready for this step, and she also knew she would never be if she didn't take it now. Her father was putting his faith in her, the same way she had put her faith in him so many times before. Even though she was afraid, she knew she could never bring herself to run away.

"When do we leave?" she asked, tightening her grip on her staff.

Thunder's answer was a simple smile, before walking outside with Tala close behind.

The trek to the Village of Three Rivers took only around three hours. Tala had been there a few times with her father and had seen it before the nuckelavee decimated it. What had once been a small fishing hamlet, nestled at the point where two rivers met and became one, was now a mess of rundown buildings. Some had broken walls, missing doors, and, in some cases, entire roofs gone. Others seemed to be rotting at the seams.

The few people out were looking through the rubble, trying to find anything they could. They wore tattered rags and seemed almost emaciated, with some of the younger adults seemingly having more bones showing than some of the others. Tala figured that they must have been skipping meals so others could eat instead.

"By the gods..." Thunder whispered.

Tala shared his sentiment and wondered how they could allow such a thing to happen. As the group of ten hunters and five wagons entered the town, some of the scavengers looked up and began to approach the group. Others ran around yelling that people had arrived, and soon, the entire remains of the village were gathered around the party. One man who seemed to be in his fifties approached, leaning heavily on a staff.

"Ah, well met, Roaring Thunder. If you've come to trade, I'm sorry to tell you that we have nothing to offer," he said, his voice sounded ragged, like someone who hasn't had much to drink.

"No, we're not here to trade, Great Willow. We've come here with an offer," Thunder replied.

"An offer?" Willow asked.

Thunder got down from his horse and stood before the haggard survivors.

"People of Three Rivers, what happened here was a tragedy. I look around and see the destruction of your village and thank the heavens themself that my village was spared from this fate. I stand before you today to offer you a chance to survive the coming winter. Come back to Wind Swept Village with us, and you shall have food, shelter, and warmth. All we ask in exchange is that you help us fortify our village and grow food for winter." Thunder spoke formally, addressing the town as a whole and not singling out any one person.

A murmur swept through the crowd. The people began to talk over each other, shouting at Thunder.

"This is our land!"

"You would have us be slaves!"

"The beast could come and attack your village next!"

Willow slammed his staff into the ground, creating a deafening boom that silenced the group.

"Your offer is appreciated, Brother Thunder, but how could we be sure of what you say? Do you have enough space for all of us? What about food? Water? How do you know the beast will not return? Understand that while you have given us no reason to mistrust you, we do need more incentive than just your word," Willow explained.

Thunder looked at Tala and smiled. Swallowing her reservations, she got down from her horse and stepped forward. All eyes from both groups fell on her as she took a deep breath.

"The idea was mine, not my father's," she said.

Another murmur swept over the survivors, this one of confusion rather than hostility.

"She's just a child."

"What are they playing at?"

"Can we really trust them?"

Tala looked to her father for support, and he replied with a nod and a gesture for her to continue. Summoning the same courage that let her face down the nuckelavee, she faced the survivors of Three Rivers and spoke loud, true, and peacefully.

"Truth be told, I don't know if this is a good idea. If I had it my way, we would steal time from the hands of Chronus himself to repair the damage that beast did to your village, but alas, that isn't an option. Our villages may have never been close enough to truly aid one another in the past, but this disaster gives us an opportunity to amend that. Winter will be difficult, no matter what, but if we don't come together, many more people could lose their lives. Your village will take months of back-breaking labor to return to any kind of livable condition, and ours may not have enough food to make it through winter," she explained.

Her announcement of the food shortage sent another rumble of concern through the crowd. Willow slammed his staff down to silence them before motioning for Tala to continue.

"If you come with us, if you help our farmers and our hunters, then all of us will be able to see spring. I admit that the first few months might not be comfortable, but you will be fed, you will be clothed, and you will be sheltered. No one will be slaves, and no one will have to fear an attack from the nuckelavee because... It's dead," Tala continued.

This statement sent a shocked gasp through the crowd, even catching Willow off guard. More murmurs began and were quickly silenced by Willow, who then turned to question Tala: "Young lady, do you intend for us to believe that you killed that foul demon?"

"No, I did. However, Tala managed to hold her own against the beast after it took down three of our most skilled hunters. She single-handedly protected our village long enough for me to arrive and deal with the threat. She and the hunters are all four heroes to our village," Thunder chimed in.

Tala nodded and added, "I am in line to become the next head chieftain, along with my future husband. I swear to all of you that under our leadership, you will be safe. Never again will you have to fear the beasts of the forest, the demons of the mountains, or the creatures that roam the night."

Another murmur arose that was stifled by Willow, who turned to his village.

"I know that it is a lot to ask. For many of us this has been our home for generations, but they do make compelling arguments. As much as I would love to watch my grandchildren grow up in the home built by my grandfather, I think that it is time for us to leave. With so few in our number, we wouldn't have the time, energy, or manpower to rebuild and reestablish our farms and fishing before winter. Anyone who is still skeptical, please speak up now, so that we may address your queries," Willow announced.

No hands were raised, though some people still looked nervous.

“Wonderful. Gather as much of your belongings as you can and stockpile them into the wagons. We have a busy day ahead,” Thunder said with a smile.

Chapter 9

As Gaius stared up at the massive, imposing mountain before him, only one thought entered his mind: *This is gonna take all fucking day.*

The mountain was roughly three miles away from the city, but it had taken Gaius only a minute or two of flying to get there. He now stood at its base, staring up to where he thought the summit should be. He felt like an ant staring up at the wall of a castle and briefly contemplated if this was worth it.

Well, I made it this far, might as well go the distance, Gaius thought with a shrug.

He took a good hard look at the wall of stones before him, looking for a hand grip.

Wait, what am I doing? I'm not trying to impress anyone.

With that thought, he quickly took off into the air, flying straight up towards the summit. After roughly three, maybe four hours, he had only made it halfway. Irritation gripped him as he saw the summit was no closer. Though he knew it could be dangerous, he decided to pick up his speed even further, shooting upward at a speed that created an explosion of air around him. He felt the strain grip his mind, as well as the sheer pain of pushing his body like this, but it was worth it. Gaius had spent most of the flight over this morning devising a genius plan that would get him the ambrosia without the risk of running afoul with the Olympians.

Stealth was his friend right now, and his biggest advantage. He was no slouch in a fight, he knew how to hold his own better than anyone else he'd ever come across, but gods were another story. While his ego told him it was possible, his brain told him it wasn't worth the risk. His best chance at survival was to sneak onto Olympus, steal a bottle of ambrosia, and be at least a few dozen miles away before they notice.

I have no idea what to do after that. I'll be a fugitive, and I don't know what to do after that. I'll have to avoid the village for a while, maybe find a cave to hide in until everything dies down.

He flew through a cloud and arrived at the top of the massive mountain. Coming to a stop created a sound like thunder, and Gaius immediately turned himself invisible. He didn't know how high the mountain was, but he could barely see the ground through the clouds.

He turned his eyes to the summit and saw a massive Parthenon. There were towers dotted around, various other small buildings were around a massive staircase that led up to the Parthenon. All of the buildings were marble white with a pristine shine, giving the whole area a bright white aura.

"Wow," Gaius said.

Gaius flew down and landed at the foot of the steps. There were multiple servants wandering around, talking, laughing, and seemingly running errands. Taking a look around, he figured that the winery would mostly be towards the top near the Parthenon. He made his way up, careful to avoid giving himself away.

He checked each building as he passed them, finding bedrooms, an armory, a kitchen and other rooms on the way up. His hypothesis was correct, as near the top, he found a building that opened up into a huge wine cellar. Magic had to be involved, as the room in the building was bigger than the outside.

Barrels lined the walls, with shelves above them lined with various bottles of liquor and wine. There was a fine red carpet on the floor that seemed to flow like wine under the lights of the hanging lanterns, and sitting in the middle of the room was a wooden table with a golden jug.

Call me paranoid, but there is definitely a trap here somewhere.

A fly buzzed by his ear, which he swatted away. It came back, buzzed by his other ear, and landed on the doorframe. Gaius quickly caught its mind and overpowered it, turning it into an extension of himself.

With a flick of his wrist, he sent the fly flying across the room to the jug. As soon as it passed the edge of the table, a spectral spear leapt up from the table and pierced right through it. The shock went through Gaius, and he cut off the connection before the pain could seep in. Taking a second to catch his breath, Gaius leaned against the wall and stared at the golden jug. He had been correct; there was definitely a trap, and that meant that there was a way to disable the trap.

Unfortunately, there weren't any other flies to send into it to see what else the trap could do. Gaius figured that the spear must've been the work of Athena, but he doubted she was the only one protecting the jug. He approached the table, cautiously, for fear of setting off another trap.

To his surprise, none activated, but he refused to drop his guard. Gaius reached the table and looked it over. The surface of the table was curved with the symbols of the twelve Olympians, as well as pictures that depicted great battles, many of which Gaius couldn't identify, but some he did.

He saw Heracles wrestling a giant, Zeus hurling lightning bolts at the massive behemoth shape of Typhon, and Perseus cutting the head from Medusa. All of these smaller carvings circled a much larger carving in the center that depicted Zeus, Hades, and Poseidon all facing down the massive figure of Cronus. Zeus was on the left, holding a lightning bolt in each hand. Hades was in the center, wielding his mighty bident and was the only one wearing a helmet. Poseidon was to his right, wielding his trident. Cronus towered over them, wielding a scythe. The jug sat on Cronus' face, a decision so spiteful it brought a small chuckle out of Gaius. He studied the artwork before him for several minutes, unaware that he had released his camouflage.

“Who are you?” a voice asked across from him.

Gaius snapped back to himself and saw a young man standing across the table from him. He was incredibly beautiful, seemingly only nineteen or twenty. He had marble white skin, with contrasting curly black hair and deep brown eyes. He wore a toga with no shirt underneath, showing off his well-toned body.

“You can’t be here. You need to leave. Now!” he said forcibly.

He took a step back as Gaius straightened back up and looked at him. Gaius stood at least a few inches taller, and tilted his head back to stare down his nose at him. The young man was trying to be brave, but Gaius could feel his fear without even needing to probe his mind.

Gaius cracked his thumb with his pointer finger, causing the young man to jump. Seizing the opportunity, Gaius lunged forward and made a grab for his face. The young man tried to get away, but stumbled and fell, giving Gaius a chance to land on him and pin him to the ground. The man went to scream, and Gaius clasped a hand on his mouth, silencing him.

“Shh... Shh... Shh...” Gaius whispered as he touched the young man’s mind.

The first thing he felt was an overwhelming fear. Gaius took a second to silence it to stop the man’s muffled screaming and squirming. Underneath that was a sadness, one that Gaius didn’t want to probe for fear he might learn something he’d regret.

He searched deep into the young man’s mind and quickly found what he was looking for. The carvings on the table acted as a lock, with a specific one in each row that disabled the entire row. There was another memory he found as well, one that showed someone’s arm impaled by the lines of spears, simply because they had hit the wrong one too far into the table. Gaius went over the memory several times, internalizing the order to avoid any unfortunate mishaps.

This entire process had taken barely a few seconds, all of it moving at the speed of thought. After he achieved what he needed, he sent a blast of psionic energy into the young man's head. There was no malice in it, only a desire to knock him unconscious. The attack was successful, and the young man was asleep before he could catch his breath.

Gaius quickly looked around for a place to hide the man's body. It took a minute, but he found an empty barrel next to the door. He took extra caution not to break anything in the young man's body, and after a few minutes, he had successfully closed the barrel on him. Gaius returned to the table and very carefully circled it, pressing each carving with a precision he hadn't known he was capable of. He finally got to the center and went to grab the bottle when the door began to open.

Shit.

Reacting at the speed of thought, Gaius quickly shimmered, moving the light around him until he resembled the young man he had put in the barrel. The door opened and a beautiful young woman wearing similar clothes with long raven black hair stood in the doorway.

"Hey, Ganymede, did you forget the combination again? The Olympians are waiting," she said.

"Oh, yeah, I'm on my way. I just finished getting it," Gaius lied, hoping he sounded like the young man.

"Okay, just hurry. You don't want Zeus to be mad at you again," she replied, walking out.

Gaius breathed a sigh of relief, only for reality to hit him. He was stuck. Now that Ganymede had been seen getting the ambrosia, they'd come looking if he didn't show up. If they looked, they'd find him unconscious in the barrel. Gaius thought quickly. He could kill Ganymede, but that would be a dead give-away as to what happened.

Plus, the young man didn't deserve it.

Gaius could live with stealing, he could even live with badly hurting someone or rewriting someone's mind, but thoughtlessly killing wasn't something he could do. He thought about erasing Ganymede's memories, but if he was found with no ambrosia, it could send all of Olympus on the hunt. He needed a better plan that would at least give him enough time to create a gap between him and the Olympians. The more he thought about it, the more it became clear he had only one real option to take. He would have to pretend to be Ganymede, serve the gods, and leave while they were distracted.

It wasn't a flawless idea, but if Ganymede was seen giving the gods the ambrosia, but not seen after, people would assume he retired for the day. It gave him time, something he didn't currently have an ample amount of. Taking a deep breath to steady himself, Gaius grabbed the jug and headed out the door, careful to keep up his disguise. He slowly climbed the steps to the Parthenon, which hung over him like a guillotine blade. This was going to be the most dangerous thing he had ever done.

The interior of the Parthenon took Gaius' breath away. Torches lined the marble walls, painting everything in a dreamy yellow light. There were twelve thrones aligned in a horseshoe shape, with two at the head and five spanning down each side. Five were empty, but seven gods sat on the remaining thrones.

At the front of the horseshoe, facing the door, was Zeus and Hera, the king and queen of the Olympians. Zeus cut an imposing figure with his white beard and gray hair. Hera had a regal poise in her golden dress and black hair. Next to Zeus sat Poseidon with his trusty trident. His goatee was neatly trimmed, and his graying hair had streaks of green running through it. Ares was a few seats away from his uncle and wore battle armor and a helmet that cast a shadow over his face. At the end of that side sat Apollo, who's beauty and elegance seemed radiant, like a blinding star.

On the side headed by Hera sat Athena and Artemis. Athena seemed to favor dull colors, with her long white dress and dull silver hair. It seemed in contrast to her sister, who wore a dark green dress and had hair as dark as midnight itself.

Gaius was dumbstruck for a second as he stared at the gods before him. He had never seen a god before, let alone ever dreaming he would meet seven. The reality of the task before him hit him in the chest. He was going to need to lie to all seven of these powerful, intimidating beings before him and escape with his life.

Great plan, genius. Maybe next you can go swimming in a volcano. You'd probably have a better chance of surviving that.

"You've finally decided to join us, Ganymede. We have serious business to discuss, and you've kept us from that," Zeus boomed.

His voice carried an authority that scared Gaius to the core. His voice carried power and prestige and once again reinforced how far out of his depth Gaius truly was.

"F-F-Forgive me, my lord. I seem to have contracted a small cold in my throat. I was getting medicine when you sent for me," Gaius replied, bowing to the gods.

He made sure to add a few coughs in between his sentences to give his lie extra credence. Zeus looked him over for a minute.

"Hmm... See that you get that taken care of. I have much better uses for your throat," Zeus answered with a wink to Poseidon.

Gaius suppressed a disgusted shudder and crossed the floor to Zeus and Hera. He poured the golden liquid into their goblets. He then began to fill Poseidon's cup as Zeus spoke again.

"Now that we have our drinks, we can begin. I was contacted by Persephone the other day, and she informed me that in a few months, it will be Hades' ten thousandth birthday. She would like to get the entire family together to celebrate," Zeus began.

Immediately, Ares, Athena, and Artemis seemed to explode in excitement. Ares clapped as Athena and Artemis began to talk to each other. Zeus slammed the bottom of his cup into the arm of his throne, silencing all three of them.

"Well, I won't be going. If I wanted to be in the underworld, I'd have married Hades millennia ago," Hera announced.

"I feel much the same. While I do love our older brother, the underworld can be rather depressing," Poseidon added.

"Yes, I thought as much. Truth be told, I hadn't planned on going either. I can guess that you three will be attending, but what of you, Apollo?" Zeus asked.

"Father, with all due respect, the sun isn't meant to shine in the underworld. Besides, Lord Hades isn't exactly my favorite relative," Apollo said, strumming across his lyre.

"There you have it. Do give Hades our regards, won't you?" Zeus addressed his question to his daughters, ignoring Ares' enthusiastic smile.

The two girls looked at each other with trepidation before Athena spoke.

"Umm... Father, I understand your problems with the underworld, but Lord Hades is your brother. And turning ten thousand is a huge milestone..." Athena began.

"What is your point, Athena?" Zeus interrupted.

Athena opened her mouth to speak, and closed it, seemingly unable to find the right words, and looked to her sister for assistance.

"I believe what Athena is trying to say is that a pack of wolves is stronger together than apart," Artemis chimed in.

Gaius had fully made a circuit around the thrones and was finally on his way to the door. Despite the fact that none of the gods acknowledged him after his entrance, he couldn't help but feel a raw tension in his gut.

This entire experience had easily been the most stressful thing he had ever done, but it was finally over.

By the gods, I did it. I actually did it. Once I get out that door, I can camouflage myself, and fly away. By the time they realize...

His inner monologue was cut off by a figure in the doorway. It was a young man, physically in his early twenties. He had piercing purple eyes and curly brown hair, from which a small set of horns protruded. He wore a loincloth made of deerskin, and had a wreath of vines around his neck.

There were small amounts of grapes growing in it, and one large one that grew down the center of his chest. He was clean-shaved, with a soft face like royalty. He held a jug in one hand, and a goblet that was raised to his lips. He had stopped mid-sip and was staring at Gaius with a curious look on his face. Then, he looked at his cup and began to laugh. It was a loud, boyish laugh that echoed through the Parthenon, pulling everyone's attention to him.

"Why do you laugh, cousin?" Apollo asked.

"Yes, share with us the meaning of this revelry so that we may enjoy it as well," Zeus boomed with a smile.

The young man strode forward and threw an arm around Gaius, pulling him forward as he continued to chuckle.

"First of all, my apologies for arriving late, Uncle Zeus. I had decided to stop by and see my old friend Ame-no-Uzume to pick up some saké for us to toast my father. I decided to drink a little on my way here, and apparently, I'm already seeing double!" the young man explained, doubling over in laughter again.

The gods looked at each other, each just as confused as the last.

"Dionysus, what is the meaning of this?" Zeus asked, his eyes boring a hole through Gaius.

Oh, no.

Dionysus straightened back up and wiped his face.

"I stopped by your wine house on my way up to top it off and found young Ganymede asleep in a barrel. I figured you had given him a rough night, and he was just sleeping it off, but here he stands, completely healthy!" Dionysus giggled as he made a pirouette away from Gaius.

I was so close...

Chapter 10

It was Ares that swung first. He must've been moving before Dionysus had finished his speech. He had closed the distance between his throne and Gaius faster than lightning itself, and was about to cleave Gaius with a large hoplite sword. The blade was as long as Gaius' torso and thicker than any sword a human would wield.

Despite the god's speed, nothing moves faster than thought. Gaius created a small wall of psychic energy in front of him to stop the attack as he began to move back. Ares' strength easily shattered the barrier, narrowly missing Gaius' nose with his swing. The sword slammed down with an impact that shook the entire mountain, causing Gaius to lose his balance and begin to fall.

As he fell, Ares lifted the sword again and stabbed at his chest. Thinking quickly, Gaius flicked his wrist and sent the sword careening to his right. Ares' look of bloodlust and joy became one of sheer confusion as he and Gaius fell towards the ground, and his sword stabbed down into the ground between Gaius' arm and chest.

Gaius smirked and brought his head up in a sharp headbutt into the war god's face, causing him to fall back.

Leaping quickly to his feet, Gaius turned to the exit and saw Artemis and Apollo standing between him and his escape. The two gods had their bows drawn and fired arrows with such speed that the entire air between them was filled with arrows before Gaius could register they were there.

Gaius quickly released a rush of psychic energy to catch the arrows. Artemis and Apollo looked at each other in utter shock, until Gaius rushed forward and delivered a drop kick to Apollo's chest. The god was caught completely unprepared and went down, gasping for breath.

Gaius quickly flipped back, turning his attention to Artemis, who had summoned a large hunting spear to her side. The blade appeared to be made of jagged bone, seemingly tied to the spear rather than forged as one piece. She rushed him first, not giving him time to attack. Like a great hunter corralling deer, she struck at him with her spear and drove him until an empty throne was behind him. She struck at him again, going for the killing blow, but Gaius dodged back, and the spear passed in front of him.

With practiced precision, he brought both his elbows down on its wooden shaft, while bringing his knee up. Artemis saw the move and began to retreat, only for the spear to become enveloped in a blue glow and slip from her hands.

Gaius finished his maneuver, snapping the shaft into three separate pieces. With a quick spin, he brought the back of his hand across Artemis' face, sending her sliding back. Before she could respond, the arrows Gaius held turned and released, flying at the goddess and forcing her to defend herself.

Gaius didn't even get a second to catch his breath before he could hear the whistle of the wind on the far side of the throne room. A war spear passed so close to his face that the wind made him blink. The spear shattered the throne and embedded itself in the wall behind it. He turned to face Athena, who smacked another spear into her shield before pointing it at Gaius, formally issuing him a challenge.

One lunge brought her right to him, causing Gaius to leap to the right to avoid her. She spun quickly, firmly putting herself between him and his escape. She lunged again, and in a flash, Gaius had summoned two spectral swords to parry her strike. The two became locked in a flurry of attacks, with Athena carefully trying to find an opening with her spear as she drove Gaius back.

Gaius, desperate and frantic, struck the spear dozens of times to parry near-fatal attacks as she drove him across the floor. In a moment of panic, Gaius swung his hand down, sending the spear stabbing into the ground. Before Athena could counter, he stepped on the spear and brought a strong right hook down into her face. Gaius wasn't much of a boxer, but his natural speed let him get off a few solid hits on Athena, two more to her face, a heavy punch to her stomach, and a jumping punch to her face, sending her careening backwards.

During the battle, the remaining gods watched with mild interest.

"He's putting up quite a fight, for a mortal," Poseidon commented.

"He's cheating. They're not using magic, but he is with no sense of honor or sportsmanship," Hera replied, taking a sip from her goblet.

"Indeed. We should teach him a lesson in manners," Zeus grumbled as he watched Gaius send Athena back.

Thunder crashed in the Parthenon, drawing everyone's attention to Zeus. Lightning flashed into being in his hands, and he pointed it at Gaius.

"I don't know who you are or what you want, but I declare you an enemy of Olympus. Give him no quarter, no matter how much he may beg for it," Zeus' voice seemed to make the walls shake with its power.

One of the few things Gaius had learned about magic was how to detect its energy. Chief Thunder had taught him that detecting the change of energy could save his life. It would let him know when someone was preparing to cast a powerful spell, or use it in some other way. He had felt Thunder use incredible power a few times before, like when he incinerated the army of draugr, but he had never felt magic like this.

There was an ocean behind him, and he was about to drown in its depths. He felt paralyzed as his mind helplessly searched for a way to reach the shore again. He could camouflage himself, run to the next and hope they didn't pursue him. He could hope Zeus was bluffing and would let

Gaius beg for mercy. His mind ran through all these ideas in a second, before another feeling emerged that took hold of his mind; pride.

Don't you get it? They see you as a threat. A challenge. If they didn't, they wouldn't be using magic. That old hag was right, this is your destiny.

The voice wasn't his own, but it felt familiar like he had heard it in a dream. While he consciously realized this wasn't the time to worry about phantom voices, he still resonated with its words. This *was* his destiny, and the gods were proving it. Finding a new resolve, he turned and faced the current behind him, resolute in the knowledge that it could try and pull him under, but it would never drown him.

The gods were back on their feet and had taken up positions for the coming battle. Apollo and Artemis had returned to the end of the hall with Ares and Athena taking arms behind Gaius. Gaius readied his swords and rushed Ares. Ares caught him by the wrist, and threw him into the center. Gaius staggered, trying to catch himself before Athena and Ares descended on him. The two of them attacked Gaius as a coordinated front, giving him no time to think, or breathe. Athena and Ares worked as a single being rather than two individuals. Ares worked a way through Gaius' defenses and quickly made an opening for Athena.

My shoulder!

Gaius quickly threw himself back, not fast enough to avoid Athena's spear, but fast enough to stop it from skewering through his shoulder entirely. Pain shot through Gaius as the spear broke flesh and sent warm blood exploding outwards.

Ares followed immediately with a long upwards slash that tore across Gaius' body, from his right hip up to his left shoulder. Before Gaius could scream in pain, the ground under his feet cracked, and an explosion of swords erupted under him.

Reacting at the speed of thought, Gaius shot into the sky, right into the line of Athena's flying spear.

What? How?

He flipped in the air, dodging the spear and transforming one of his swords into a spear. He threw it at Athena, who sidestepped it, before it exploded with blue energy right next to her. Athena wasn't expecting it, and the blast sent her flying back. Ares had leapt into the air while Gaius was distracted and grabbed his leg.

With incredible strength, he swung Gaius downwards, aiming to skewer him on the swords. Gaius narrowly caught himself above the swords, only for Ares to swing and throw him towards the far wall, bouncing him off it with incredible force. Artemis' shot an arrow and pinned his hand in place, leaving him dangling ten feet off the ground. The pain was damn near blinding, and it took every ounce of willpower for Gaius to keep from blacking out.

As the four gods regrouped, Gaius had a few seconds to think of a plan. He didn't have enough information to guess how they were using their magic, and Artemis and Apollo seemed content to stay back and apply support while Ares and Athena did the actual fighting.

Gaius thought back to his lessons with Thunder and what the gods were known for. Ares and Artemis were war gods, that much was obvious.

Artemis was a moon goddess, as well as a goddess of the hunt. Apollo was the god of the sun, as well as music and medicine. So far as Gaius knew, none of his domains had to do with combat, meaning he was the weakest link of the four. And with enough pressure, any link is capable of breaking.

The gods crossed the hall to Gaius as Dionysus offered a small round of applause. They looked at each other for a second, seeming to see who would move first. Athena chose to take the initiative.

"Do you yield, mortal?" she asked.

Gaius nodded, refusing to lift his head.

"Speak, or we'll turn you into a quiver for our arrows," Ares growled.

Anger began to grow in Gaius' chest. Despite his prowess, they still refused to look at him as anything more than a mortal. He had given his all in this battle, and he deserved, no, demanded their respect.

You haven't given your all. Not yet.

It was the phantom in his head again. Once again, it was right. The only problem was that if Gaius used everything he was capable of, it could kill him. Gaius telekinesis could easily tax his mind, and if he wasn't careful, it could easily cause his brain to hemorrhage.

You won't die. Remember, you're destined to bring forth a great change. In order for that to happen, you will have to live. You will have to fight.

The words rang true to what the old woman had told him. He needed that ambrosia, he needed these gods out of the way. He needed to stop holding back. But he couldn't just let his power run wild, that was something children did. He needed his mind to focus.

The entire Parthenon began to shake, causing even the seated gods to take notice. Gaius had kept his head down for a second and snapped it upwards, allowing the gods to see the blue energy pouring from his eyes. The wall behind him exploded inwards, sending rubble flying inwards and filling the Parthenon with a cloud of dust and dirt, sending the gods scrambling. Gaius was going to need to be fast. He could already feel his head beginning to throb. He quickly took off towards the center, where he had dropped the jug of ambrosia.

"The ambrosia!" Athena yelled over the confusion.

Through the dust, Gaius could make out the shape of a man holding a bow. Following on his theory, he clenched a fist and threw it forward, launching a barrage of rubble at Apollo. He saw the figure notch an arrow and shoot it.

As the arrow sailed through the debris, Gaius soon remembered another aspect of Apollo's domains: archery. Gaius' debris hit their mark, and he narrowly moved Apollo's arrow from its target: his heart. Gaius quickly realized the arrowhead was on fire, and barely had time to conjure a dome around him before the fire swirled and formed a small sun. Gaius threw his hands up, both to cover his eyes and try to force the mini star away. Gaius screamed in pain as his hands began to burn from the heat, and felt the blood begin to ooze from his nose.

In an instant, the star vanished, temporarily dazzling Gaius with the change in lighting and giving Ares an opening to leap from the dust cloud and drive his sword down in a powerful swing.

Reacting at the speed of thought, Gaius focused his energy around his hand, creating a small barrier that stopped the attack, but brought him to his knees.

Ares began to pound away at the barrier, an obvious distraction for whatever Athena was doing behind Gaius. He spun his head quickly to look behind him, only to see a pack of spectral wolves emerge from the dust in the direction of the ambrosia.

Whipping his head back to face them, he didn't see Ares spin and deliver a massive kick to his exposed chest. He was sent sprawling towards the wolves which immediately rushed him, attacking with a flurry of bites and scratches.

Gaius covered his face as they ripped at his arms and chest, with one of them going right for his leg and ripping a massive gash into his calf muscle. Through the confusion, he saw movement above him in the dust, and moved his head just in time to avoid Athena diving down with her spear.

The spear stabbed an inch from his ear, and she landed hard on his chest, knocking the breath clean from his lungs. Gaius thrusted a fist upwards and yanked back down, causing the ceiling to collapse above them.

Athena looked up and quickly leapt away, leaving the rubble to fall on Gaius. Gaius caught it and whipped it around him in a cyclone, shattering the spectral wolves and causing any nearby gods to scramble away.

Gaius brought himself to his feet and could see the gods circling him outside of his impromptu barrier. Gathering what was left of his energy, Gaius threw his arms out to his sides, sending a massive blast of blue energy from himself that cleared the area around him and sent the debris flying in various directions.

The gods were fast enough to dodge the rubble with no difficulty, but the force of the energy blast sent them all flying. In the few seconds he had earned, Gaius began to limp over to the bottle of ambrosia. It was his only goal at this point, and adrenaline pushed him to it with as much speed as his wounded body could muster.

In steps that were an awkward mix between a drunk limp and full on running, he managed to get to the jug. Dropping to his knees, he reached out for it, and an arrow tore through his hand again, pinning it in place. Gaius let out a scream of pain and broke the arrow before jumping to his feet and turning to face the four gods again.

They were directly behind him, and Gaius realized he had made a mistake; the current could drown him. Gaius clenched a fist and threw it forward, but nothing happened. His head screamed in an unholy pain as his vision began to blur, and he fell to all fours.

This was it, it was over.

His arms and chest were covered in gashes and bite marks, Ares had broken a few ribs with his kick, he couldn't get his breath back, his arms and hands were covered in flash burns and blisters from Apollo's sun magic, and he was pretty sure that bastard had broken his nose when he headbutted him.

Wait... No.

No one had headbutted Gaius. Gaius had headbutted... Ares. The realization sent a shock through Gaius' system as he felt the side of Artemis' face still stinging from his hit, the bruises forming under Athena's armor, and the various cuts the rubble had caused on Apollo. He had made contact with all of the gods here, and accidentally linked their minds to his own.

Gaius could utilize his telepathy through force, by digging into something's mind and forcing it to yield to him, or passively by making contact with something. One that activated through touch didn't drain as much of Gaius' strength, and was completely invisible to the target so long as Gaius didn't make himself known. He was so focused on surviving the battle he didn't realize he had been able to read their minds the entire time.

Gods, I'm such an idiot, he thought to himself. *If only I had realized sooner, maybe I wouldn't be about to die.*

The gods closed in on him, and Gaius rose to his knees, facing them head on. Hollow laughter echoed through his mind.

Who is that?

Don't worry about who I am right now, would you like some help?

It was the voice again, and it was mocking him. Gaius couldn't muster the energy to be annoyed, so he simply replied, *How could you help me?*

You really want to know?

By all means, it's not like I have many other choices.

So, you were always a smartass.

Before Gaius could register any confusion, energy exploded through his mind, catching him completely by surprise. He was still in incredible pain, but at least he could defend himself. As the gods approached, he pulled himself to his feet and faced them again. The pain was so unbearable that his vision blurred with tears. The pain caused an idea to spring forth in Gaius' mind, and he scanned through his body for every injury he could find. He felt every muscle scream, every vessel and bone that was broken, every nerve that cried from the stress, and he let the feelings wash through him.

Then he sent it right into the minds of the gods.

The results were immediate. Apollo let out a high-pitched, ear-splitting scream before clutching his head and falling to his knees. Ares fully stopped as his eyes began to twitch, and he fell flat on his face. Athena grabbed at her head and doubled over as tears fell from her eyes. Artemis completely dropped to the floor with no fanfare, but Gaius could see the tears beginning to pool by her face.

"What's happening?" Zeus roared.

Taking his opening, Gaius grabbed the jug and began to sprint for the door. Poseidon was on top of him in an instant, but Gaius was ready. He focused all of his pain into a sharpened spear, and with practice precision, drove it into Poseidon's mind. The god crumbled immediately, roaring with a ferocity that shook the Parthenon.

On top of his roar, another echoed through, forcing Gaius to look over his shoulder. Zeus was on his feet and had a lightning bolt in his hand. He reared back and threw it like a javelin, dead set on skewering this intruder. Then, something happened that Gaius couldn't explain.

Time itself seemed to slow. The lightning bolt was traveling incredibly slow, giving Gaius enough time to turn and face it. There was no dodging it or sending it off course, as it was already too close to him.

Thankfully, while everything seemed to move slowly, Gaius could still move at his regular speed. He reached out and caught the bolt before it could hit his chest. The impact sent him skidding backwards several feet, before he was about to force himself to stop. He could see the stunned looks on the faces around him as he raised it up like a javelin.

Lightning ripped through his arm, leaving burning gashes that showed the muscle under as he took his aim. With a ferocious roar rivaled by none in all the realms, Gaius pulled back his arm and through the bolt.

It sailed true, and slammed into the wall behind Zeus, passing right by his head as it did so.

In the second of stunned confusion, Gaius camouflaged himself and raced to the door. Once he was through, he flung himself into the air and rocketed away as fast as he could.

To his surprise, the energy that the voice had granted him carried him until nightfall. He landed in the forest and collapsed. The world seemed to throb with his head, and he could feel the blood oozing from different parts of his body.

With as much strength as he could manage, he pulled himself into a sitting position against a tree and sat panting as the night air cooled his body. It only lasted for a second though, as his adrenaline began to wear off. It was blocking most of the pain, which quickly rushed over Gaius and caused him to cry out in agony. It felt like death was at his door, and he needed to do something about it.

Forcing himself to move, he uncorked the bottle of ambrosia and raised it to his lips. He tilted his head back to drink and saw the beautiful full moon staring down at him. As he looked on at its beauty, he thought of one of the first pieces of history Thunder had taught him: the story of Chang'e.

In the distant past, Chang'e and her husband Hou Yi were exiled from the Court of Heaven after a miscommunication resulted in the death of a number of the Jade Emperor's sons. Neither of them wanted to remain mortal, so Hou Yi embarked on a quest and found a woman with a potion of immortality.

After telling the story of his fall from heaven, the woman gave them the potion with a warning: the fruit used for it only bloomed once every thousand years, so they wouldn't be able to obtain a second one. She told Hou Yi that drinking half of the potion would make someone immortal, but the full thing would grant them divinity.

Dismayed, Hou Yi returned home to Chang'e, and the two agreed that they didn't want to live forever without their divine powers, so the potion was hidden away in their home.

After a few years, the two were living fruitful lives. Hou Yi had decided to put his archery skills to use and teach people the proper way to wield a bow and hunt. However, one of his apprentices overheard them discussing the potion one day and waited until Hou Yi was out hunting to attack Chang'e.

During the struggle, the potion's location was revealed, and Chang'e took an arrow to her chest to protect it. In an attempt to save both herself and any others the apprentice might hurt, Chang'e drank the entire potion, returning to her original divinity. She ascended to the Court of Heaven, but was firmly told to leave, as she was still banished.

So, she made her home on the moon, where she could watch over Hou Yi as he grew old. Hou Yi left her out offerings and stayed loyal to his wife until the end of his life.

As the moon stared down at him, Gaius felt sorrow grip his heart. Tala was the love of his life, the only woman he had ever wanted to be with. She made his days better just by being around him. He loved her laugh, her smile, and the way that the two of them simply seemed to click together. He thought about how they could sit down and do nothing together, or simply talk about their day as time slipped by them. She was his everything, and now that he knew she felt the same way about him, could he really leave her like that? Would he really want to live forever without her? No, he decided that his future would be with her, no matter what.

He didn't know how much ambrosia was in the bottle, but he decided to drink down three swallows of it. It was sweet, but it burned on the way down. The warmth slowly spread through his body, and he began to feel his pain disappear.

He looked at his arms and stared in awe as new skin covered the bruises, burns, and gashes that covered them from shoulder to fingertips. He could feel his bones shift around and mend back together and could feel the incredible pain in his head slowly vanish. He felt as physically healthy as he had that morning, but it did nothing for his overall exhaustion. This had been a long, though fruitful, day. He leaned his head back against the tree and closed his eyes.

Before he faded into unconsciousness, however, one thought passed through his mind. *How have I not been found yet?*

Chapter 11

"Find him! Find him! Find him!" Zeus screamed as the other gods brought themselves back to their feet.

It had only been a minute since Gaius had left. The pain he had inflicted on the gods seemed to have ended, though a few of them still felt its lingering effects. In the heat of the moment, none of them had seen the brief exchange between Gaius and Zeus, who seemed utterly shaken.

"ON! YOUR! FEET! WE NEED TO FIND HIM!" Zeus' face was turning crimson in his rage.

Though she could barely understand what was happening, Athena saw her father's rage and quickly leapt to her feet, only to immediately drop to her knees in pain again. Ares forced himself upright, but his vision was too blurry to focus. Apollo, unaccustomed to physical combat, was completely paralyzed by the pain and lay there, weeping like a child. Artemis was able to bring herself up, but found difficulty balancing. Poseidon's ears were ringing too much to hear Zeus' yells, and he struggled to simply sit himself upright.

"USELESS! ALL OF YOU!" Zeus roared again, stepping down from his throne.

Dionysus stood up and crossed in front of him, stopping him from whatever it was he was about to do.

"Uncle, with all due respect, please calm down. He is only one man, and he was badly injured in the fight. There is no way he'll be able to get very far," Dionysis explained calmly.

`"Yes, though the Buddha will be upset with us, it isn't like he won't be found. Who knows, maybe he already has been? Buddha sees all, right?

Plus, Odin has those pesky ravens of his always poking around," Hera added.

This seemed to cause Zeus to relax somewhat.

"Yes, you have a point. We will simply need to explain that he fought unfairly and had more tricks than we were expecting. Still, I would rather our seating with the Buddha not be marred by ineptitude. When you recover, the four of you will commence searching for him," Zeus replied.

He headed back to his throne, and by the time he sat down, his four children were gone. Poseidon was on his feet finally, and crossed the floor back to his throne.

"Do you really think they'll find him?" he asked.

"If he hasn't already been found, those four will have the best odds of any of us," Zeus replied, resting his cheek on his fist.

"There is one thing I struggle to grasp though," Hera said.

"And what would that be?" Zeus grumbled.

"How is it that a mortal man scaled Olympus, stole our ambrosia, and didn't have every single god, goddess, and immortal being in the nine realms descending upon us in a righteous fury that would tremble the World Tree to its very roots?" Hera asked, swirling her drink in its glass.

Zeus and Poseidon looked to each other as the realization washed over them.

"She has a point, it doesn't make any sense," Poseidon mumbled, rubbing his head.

"The Buddha... Should have seen him," Zeus' words hung in the air with a weight like the sky itself.

Athena's chariot streaked across the sky, close behind her sister's. Artemis followed her spectral wolves as they raced forward. The wolves suddenly stopped and started to sniff around.

"What's wrong?" Athena called over the wind.

"I don't know, it seems like they lost the smell. But that's not possible. My magic can track anything or anyone to the underworld and back," Artemis called back.

"This day is getting more and more bizarre," Athena said as her chariot pulled up beside Artemis'.

"I know, I can't wrap my head around any of this. We had him against the wall, and he suddenly inflicted pain on us without touching us. None of this makes any sense to me," Artemis replied, watching the wolves closely.

Athena nodded, her eyes scanning the sky with a far-away look in her eyes.

"None of this is sitting right with me. Even with magic, we should've been able to see him coming. And the fact that we haven't found him yet... something's wrong here," Athena absentmindedly ran a hand through her hair as she spoke.

"It's a bad sign when a goddess of wisdom is confused," Artemis mumbled.

Apollo's chariot streaked above them and came to a halt before swinging back around and descending in front of them.

"Any sign of him?" he asked.

Artemis explained the situation, and Apollo delivered his own news, "I can't find him either, I've flown over Midgard twice. Father isn't going to be thrilled."

Artemis and Athena glanced at each other. Though he'd never admit it, they knew Zeus treated his sons harsher than his daughters, so they had no reason to fear him.

"Yes, he will surely deliver some punishment on us," Artemis replied dryly.

Athena couldn't help but smirk at that. Apollo sighed before turning his chariot around and speeding off.

They searched until the sun began to set.

"Oh no. This isn't good," Artemis' voice was tinged with desperation as she searched the ground below her.

Athena didn't reply, merely scanning the horizon for any scrap she could find. The two goddesses turned at the sound of frantic flapping wings, like a hummingbird fleeing from a cheetah. A young man, physically in his late teens, flew towards them and came to a stop before them. He had wavy brown hair, deep brown eyes, and a clean-shaven face. He wore a clean white toga, and a hat and sandals that both had wings on them. In his left hand, he carried a staff that had two snakes wrapped around it and another set of wings on top of it.

"Greetings, dear sisters! Father has requested your audience, Athena, for the upcoming Pantheon Council. And he also wanted Artemis to get back to work," he said, bowing in an exaggerated manner.

"Hello Hermes, nice to see you too," Artemis growled in annoyance.

"Yes, I thought as much. Please tell him I'll be there in a few minutes," Athena answered, a similar annoyed look on her face.

Hermes bowed with a smirk, then sped off in the direction he came from.

"Well, I guess I had better get back to work. Good luck, and we'll have to meet up in a few weeks to coordinate our present for Uncle's birthday," Artemis said, grabbing the reins to her chariot.

"Of course, our favorite uncle will need a truly memorable gift for his ten thousandth birthday. The only question is, what?" Athena replied before her chariot streaked off towards Olympus.

She arrived at the Parthenon in only five minutes and found Zeus standing outside, running a hand through his beard.

"This is not going to be a good day. I was hoping we'd be able to deal with this problem before things escalated to the Council," Zeus grumbled as he got into Athena's chariot.

“Yes, well, this whole day has been an exciting experience for all of us. Hopefully, Buddha will understand and not treat us too harshly,” Athena replied as she shook the reins.

The two streaked off into the sky, either one too confident in what the night held for them.

Chapter 12

The Pantheon Council was the single largest event in all the realms. It is held every one hundred years, and is attended by the head of each pantheon, their most trusted advisor, and the Buddha himself.

Each meeting was meant to bring pantheons together, promote unity, and pass any needed legislation to limit or prevent current or future problems. The last meeting had been sixty years ago, where it was almost unanimously agreed to pass the Heracles Accords, a law that forbade any gods from siring demi-god children with mortals. This was the first emergency meeting to be held in five hundred years, the cause of that meeting being the unethical way Isis had usurped power of the Egyptian pantheon from Ra. Though it was ultimately decided that her methods weren't entirely favorable, she was more fit to lead than Ra, and many of the other gods in their pantheon.

While Zeus would never have said it out right, he always hated these meetings. They would sometimes take many days, with the first one simply involving one of Buddha's disciples prattling off a list of all the gods in attendance. There were multiple alliances forged secretly in the background, an unfortunate consequence of democracy. There would be arguments about what should be made a law, what shouldn't, then the long and arduous task of every pantheon leader voting yes or no, and Zeus hoped that he would never have to experience another tie like when they tried to pass the Anansi Accords.

The Anansi Accords would've forbidden any god from using magic or trickery to deceive and win a bet or challenge, and it resulted in three years of debates, recounts, and underhanded tactics that would've made the accords namesake blush. Much to Zeus' delight, however, when it was finally over, the accord did not pass and he was still free to do what he pleased.

Many of these memories and thoughts passed through Zeus' head as Athena streaked across the sky in her chariot. Athena's mind seemed to be elsewhere as she steered the chariot. As they ascended higher, the world beneath them grew in size as Athena began to circle the massive trunk of Yggdrasil, the World Tree.

Yggdrasil was massive, holding the full weight of all the realms on its branches, with Midgard growing around its trunk. Zeus imagined that the sight of the massive tree and the realms around it must be fascinating to anyone who didn't see it as often as gods do. The Buddha had a temple perched at the highest point of Yggdrasil, and from it you could see the entire tree, and, allegedly, even Atlas and the Pillars of Eternity, if your eyesight was good enough.

"A violation of any one of the accords is almost unheard of," Athena said, seemingly just airing out her mind rather than talking to Zeus directly.

"Yes, at least that's what we're told. Truthfully, I wouldn't put it past Odin to have broken a couple himself." Zeus grumbled.

"Yes... *Odin* has definitely broken some," Athena replied sarcastically.

"Young lady, I don't need your sass right now. My personal business is my own, and I'd appreciate it if you kept your nose out of it," Zeus' voice had a hard edge to it, which quickly shut down any more conversation.

The remaining journey was held in silence. Athena knew she had crossed a line, but she didn't care. Her father could be a real pain in the ass, and she was the only one who would call him out when he started to act too high and mighty.

She knew it was risky; if she pushed against him too hard he might lash out like a child. She had seen him do it to Hera, Poseidon, and even Hestia when she tried to give him advice. While it was never explicitly stated on Olympus, Athena knew the other gods saw her as Zeus' keeper, the only person who could check Zeus' attitude and deal with his anger.

It took some time for the temple to come into view. It stood at least twenty floors high, and had two large statues of Buddha in front of the large wooden door on the bottom floor. Each floor was outlined in a balcony with several large doors and windows that opened to them. There were a few small towers that surrounded the large central temple. Monks could be seen walking the balconies, and praying in the courtyard. Various other chariots were parked by the gate to the courtyard.

"We're not the first ones here," Zeus observed.

"I would assume others weren't out looking, so they got here sooner," Athena replied as she brought the chariot down to a landing.

"Another smart remark?" Zeus asked.

"No, just an observation," Athena replied, solemnly.

They walked through the courtyard. The monks kept their heads bowed as they chanted their sutras, some of which Athena knew from her studies, others she had only heard in passing. There were two monks standing by the door who bowed to Zeus and Athena as they approached.

"Welcome, Lord Zeus and Lady Athena," they said in unison.

Athena bowed in response, but Zeus merely nodded an acknowledgement to them. The monks pushed open the door for them, and they entered the massive bottom floor of the temple. Zeus and Athena had never been here for anything but a council meeting, so they didn't know what the temple typically looked like, but they were more than familiar with its current setup. Three long tables were set in the shape of a u with a large set of steps leading to the second floor in its center. There were various gods and goddesses seated around already, each one talking loudly and aggressively.

Zeus released an agitated sigh as they walked around the table to find a seat. Once they sat down, everything went silent.

The Buddha had appeared at the top of the steps with a vibrant smile on his face. Next to him stood a tall, muscular monkey with brown fur and golden hair. His eyes shone bright red, like burning coals. He wore a kilt made of tiger skin, and a golden crown on his head. He smiled jovially, and had his arms behind his head.

Zeus swallowed at the sight of him. Sun Wukong rarely appeared at these meetings, only arriving in a time of crisis. He hadn't even appeared at the meeting about Isis, so to appear at this one had to mean that even the Buddha was concerned.

Sun Wukong had a reputation like no other, having rampaged through the Palace of Heaven, battled various demons and monsters, and even clashed with several gods and goddesses at this very table, along with their most powerful champions. The two walked down the stairs, and all of the gods and goddesses rose to their feet and bowed.

"Welcome, everyone. As I'm sure that you're aware, we have a problem on our hands that needs to be addressed. A mortal has somehow obtained ambrosia and has used it to obtain divinity, thus violating the Wukong Accords," the Buddha began.

Sun Wukong's tail flicked at the mention of his name. A woman with dark skin and long black braids cascading down to her lower back stood up. Her vibrant blue eyes pierced through those she gazed upon. She wore a golden crown with a large red disk that stood high on her head. She wore a white cloth shirt that covered her chest, but exposed her stomach and strong abs. Her legs were covered with a white skirt that went down to her knees. She wore a cape of red and blue feathers that hung down to her knees.

At her side stood Thoth, a tall god of equally dark complexion whose head was that of an ibis. He wore a no shirt, but wore a kilt of gold and white. She bowed before Buddha, who appeared slightly taken aback.

"The floor recognizes Lady Isis of Egypt," the Buddha said, motioning for her to speak.

"Thank you, Lord Buddha. With all due respect, I don't understand how this is a problem for anyone but the Olympians. It is their failure and incompetence that has brought this problem on," Isis explained.

An older man with gray hair and a gray beard stood up next to her. He had an eyepatch covering his left eye, and his right one was a deep blue, like the ocean during a storm. He wore a crown with large metal wings that protruded off it. He wore a chain link shirt with a brown robe underneath it. At his side stood Tyr, a tall man with brown hair and beard who wore full Viking battle armor, and still appeared formidable, despite missing his right hand.

"The floor recognizes Lord Odin of Asgard," the Buddha said, motioning for him.

"Isis, you may not realize this, but any violation of the accords, if left unpunished, could be the start of our entire system failing," Odin said.

"Isis wouldn't care, she loves to destroy any system that has any semblance of structure," Zeus yelled out of turn.

"At least *I'm* not such a fool as to get an accord passed because of my actions, Zeus," Isis snapped back.

"Maybe if anyone wanted to sleep with you, you'd have more children," Zeus retorted, his face hardening.

"Oh it's always about a woman's sexual appeal with you, you disgusting shape-shifting rapist pig!" Isis snarled.

"Easy, everyone. We're here to have a civilized discussion," Buddha said, raising his hands.

"These brutes wouldn't know civilized conversation if it slapped them in the face." An Asian man with a long black beard yelled.

He wore a long robe of green and a hat with horns on it. Next to him stood The Gold Star of Venus, an older Asian man in a white robe with a long white beard.

"Oh, and the Jade Emperor, who struggles to keep his own pantheon's *pets* in check, would like to educate *me* on civilized conversation. My people invented our entire governing system, and you wish to call us brutes!" Zeus yelled, leaping to his feet.

Everything quickly devolved into screaming and yelling at that point. Various gods screamed about anything, blame was thrown, old grudges were brought up and thrown at others.

"Everyone, please," Buddha said, raising his hands.

No one listened, or seemingly even heard him speak. With a look of desperation, Buddha turned to Sun, who sighed in annoyance. He reached up and pulled something from behind his ear.

With a shake of his wrist, the thing in his hands grew into a large staff that was red down the shaft with two golden tips that had carvings of the sea and sky. He slammed it into the ground, creating a sound like an explosion that immediately silenced the entire room. The gods all looked at him and the air in the temple filled with a palpable tension.

"That's enough. The next god to speak out of turn will get a taste of old Monkey's rod. This situation affects us all and Lord Buddha has a plan to solve it," Sun's voice carried more authority than almost anyone else in the room.

All gods who were standing immediately sat down, and all arguments seemed to immediately be settled.

"Thank you, Victorious Buddha. Now, contrary to what was just said, I do not actually have a plan," Buddha said, clapping his hands.

Sun's jaw hung open as the shock swept through the room.

"Yes, yes, I know. But the truth is, despite my ability to see everything in the universe, whoever this person is I cannot see them," Buddha explained.

"I had a similar problem with my ravens and Heimdall," Odin added.

"Yes, despite the best efforts of my hunting party, they searched all day and could not find him," Zeus added.

"Yes, this is quite an anomaly. So, does anyone have any ideas that could draw him out?" Buddha asked.

No one spoke up. So, Athena stepped forward and cleared her throat.

"Ah, of course. The floor recognizes Lady Athena of Olympus," Buddha said, motioning to Athena with a smile.

Athena bowed in response and began, "I've been thinking, whoever this person is, it seems like his ultimate goal was to obtain godhood. And if that was the case, I ask you then, where is he? Why is he not standing before us, demanding that we bow to him?"

"Is there a point here?" the Jade Emperor interjected.

"I'm getting to it. Ambrosia can grant full godhood when an entire goblet is consumed, but grants immortality when half a goblet is drunk. I believe he only drank half a serving, and might be saving the last half for someone else," Athena explained.

Tyr piped up"That's actually an acute observation."

Athena smiled and bowed at the recognition before continuing, "I feel like whatever it is that is keeping him hidden couldn't possibly be able to affect someone else. He's going to be hiding for a while, waiting for us to stop searching for him. So, if we wait for him to give the ambrosia to whoever it is, we should be able to find them and, by extension, him as well."

A small murmur went across the council as many of the gods seemed to agree. Athena felt a brief moment of triumph, which was cut short by the harsh mocking laughter of the Jade Emperor.

"Oh, yes, excellent plan. Let's just sit around and wait for him to hypothetically give the other half of the ambrosia to some mystery person somewhere in the realms. Meanwhile, this wanted criminal who no one seems to be able to find can just walk the realms and do whatever he pleases with no warden to report to. I can't possibly see a flaw in such a wonderfully logical plan. Let me ask you, Athena, what is your plan if this is wrong? What if he's simply waiting for the pressure to die down and start attacking some of the weaker pantheons? What if he's out there right now, causing untold havoc and destruction in who knows where?" the Jade Emperor's words seemed to change the tide of the conversation.

The murmur around the council was now filled with doubt. Despite his best efforts to unnerve her, however, Athena stood her ground. She had run through every possibility earlier that day as she composed this strategy.

"To your points, Emperor, there are more than enough ways for us to track any destruction he might try to cause. Heimdall can survey all of the realms at once, there are various sun gods who watch over Midgard, Odin's ravens cover all of the realms in less than an hour, and Buddha himself can see everything happening at all times. If he were going to try and attack any pantheon, he would've done it before we were all aware of his presence and his crime. I admit that letting a wanted criminal who is now immortal roam free for however long it takes isn't the best idea, but unless you have a better plan, it's the best one we have," Athena explained.

"And how, pray tell, will you catch him before he has a chance to flee again?" the Jade Emperor asked.

Sun Wukong cleared his throat, a sound that came from beside the Buddha, despite Sun himself suddenly being in front of the Jade Emperor, who yelped in surprise and almost fell out of his seat.

"Are you doubting the speed of old Monkey, my friend?" Sun asked.

The Jade Emperor cleared his throat, straightened his robe, and clasped his hands in front of him, despite the slight chuckle from the Gold Star at his side.

"I would never, I've seen what you're capable of first-hand, my little Pi-Ma-Wen," the Jade Emperor sneered.

Sun stepped back and crossed his arms, an action that sent a wave of fear through the council. Since his journey with Tripitaka and becoming a Buddha, Sun had become much calmer, but no one doubted he could easily wreak havoc against all of the realms.

The Underworld still hadn't fully repaired from when Sun, Anansi, Loki, and Coyote had gone out partying, and that was almost three millennia ago. To openly mock Sun with the title he hated the most was almost unheard of. Thor had done it once, on a dare, and the resulting punch had leveled an entire mountain range, and left Thor bedridden for several months.

"Given the urgency of the situation at hand, old Monkey is willing to let this slide, but remember that my heavenly title is The Victorious Fighting Buddha now," Sun said, his voice carrying an edge that shook the council to its foundation.

"Now, now, I know tensions are high right now, but there's no reason to be hostile with each other. We're all friends here, and no one wants a fight," the Buddha said, walking forward.

He placed a calm, but assertive, hand on Sun's shoulder and led him back to the center of the room.

"Back to the subject at hand, Lady Athena's plan is our best option. Heimdall is always surveying the realms and alerting us to any problems at hand, and with Hugin and Munin we can easily get word out to the other pantheons before he has a chance to escape," Tyr said, trying to defuse the tension in the air.

"Here's a thought: has anyone tried to scry for him or track him down with magic?" Isis asked, standing back up again.

"My sister Artemis—," Athena began.

"The hunting goddess?" Isis interrupted.

"Yes, the hunting goddess. She used her magic to try and track him down. We lost the trail a few miles away from Olympus," Athena concluded.

"So, you didn't think to try having a goddess of magic use any kind of scrying or anything to find him?" Isis asked.

"Well, no. We figured he wouldn't have been able to get too far," Athena replied.

Isis let out a short bark of laughter.

"I'm surrounded by fools. Did you happen to get a fragment of cloth or something from him?" Isis asked.

"I stabbed him in the shoulder with my spear," Athena replied, summoning the spear to her side.

The tip of it was covered in dry blood. Isis walked around the table and waved her hand, causing dry blood to flake from the spear and fly to her hands. The blood hovered over her palm, rotating for a second before Isis closed her eyes. The energy in the room shifted as a spectral model of Yggdrasil and all the realms appeared before Isis. She flicked her wrist, sending the blood into the air.

"Find him," she whispered.

The blood hovered above the spectral display for a few seconds before flying back to Isis' hand. Isis' eyes shot open in shock.

"What's wrong Isis? Couldn't find him?" Zeus asked, mockingly.

Odin clapped sarcastically as he rose to his feet. He walked around the table and stood on the other side of the model from Isis.

"Isis my dear, you may have the true name of Ra, but I hung myself from the World Tree itself and have been blessed with knowledge you couldn't even dream of," Odin laughed as he pulled the blood to himself.

He raised his hand and summoned a spear. The handle was long and carved with intricate runes and the spear tip was a brilliant shining silver color that looked like it was made of liquid. He took the blood in his hand and touched it to the tip of the spear. The spear tip began to pulse a red light, and Odin leaned it towards the spectral model. There was a spark of blue light for a second, then black energy began to ooze out over the model and destroy it. Everyone watched on in stunned silence.

"What do you think that means?" Tyr asked.

Odin's eye stared at the dissipating model and said nothing. He walked around the table and sat back down. Tyr looked at him questioningly, and Odin shot him a look that silenced it.

"Yes, well, if Lady Isis is done trying to prove whatever point it is that she's on, we can get back to trying to find and stop this criminal," the Jade Emperor said snarkily.

"There's nothing left for us to try. We can't scry him, we can't see him, all we can truly do is wait," Zeus grumbled.

"Yes, it would seem that this is unfortunately where this meeting comes to an end. Every path before us is closed, so we simply must see how things play out," Buddha replied.

With a clap of his hands the doors to the monastery opened and one by one, each god pairing made their way outside to their chariots, though some were in better moods than others.

Chapter 13

Thoth merely guided the chariot as Isis ranted behind him. He was more than familiar with this very one-sided conversation, as she had had it after every council meeting. Isis wasn't liked by the majority of the council for the way she had come into power.

When Ra had started to get older, he began to lose his mind and the Egyptians began to lose their standing within the council. In an act of, in her words at least, "desperation", she stole some of Ra's saliva and molded it with clay, creating a small snake that bit Ra on the heel.

Egypt was built by Ra, and nothing in it could hurt him as a result, but the clay snake was made from Ra, giving it power to hurt him. Isis used the opportunity to convince Ra to give her his true name, giving her power over him and Egypt itself.

This understandably caused many gods and goddesses who control their pantheons through what they deemed "legitimate" means exceptionally angry. Zeus and Odin, both of whom obtained power through trial and bloodshed, despised Isis and saw her as nothing but a power hungry witch who they couldn't turn their backs on.

Isis fought hard to be seen as their equal, but it was clear, to Thoth at least, that they were never going to accept her. It wasn't her fault, she was a woman, and much like Pele and Amaterasu, she was deemed as nothing but a pretty face who should remain silent. Isis knew this, and refused to follow the path of the other two.

While they were respected in their own pantheons, the council at large viewed them as faces to admire and voices to silence. Isis, however, refused to be silenced. Thoth thought it was her best, and worst, quality.

Thoth's mind was adrift with the events from the meeting. He knew Odin would be knocking at his door shortly, and they would have much to discuss, but the topic of the meeting wasn't what his mind was on.

"And don't even get me started on that immature, self-centered, egotistical, misogynistic rapist pig!" Isis yelled.

Thoth saw a chance to quickly interject and took it.

"My Lady, may I speak freely?" Thoth asked.

Isis sighed and waved a hand for him to speak.

"With all due respect, you're not Lord Ra," he began.

Isis looked surprised and went to respond, but Thoth held up his hand to silence her.

"Lord Ra was respected because he battled Apophis and banished him, on top of being a sun god. To the gods on the council, he was seen as a great warrior and king. You are seen as a witch, a traitor, and a usurper.

"For the last five centuries, I served as your advisor, just as I did for Lord Ra, and have watched you struggle to force them to see you as an equal. To be frank, it has been pitiful, for we both know it will never happen. Men like Zeus and the Jade Emperor refuse to acknowledge women as their equals, and Odin will always try to prove he is a better magician than you. I know that you refuse to go the way of Amaterasu and Pele, which is why I would like to propose a change in action," Thoth explained.

"Which would be?" she asked.

"Originally, my plan was to stage a way for another god to seemingly rise to power in our pantheon. I thought that perhaps he could send your son Horus to round up Set so we could imprison him once and for all, and as a reward you would step down and—," Thoth began.

"You would have me give up my throne?!" Isis yelled as magic began to swirl around her.

"Not at all, Your Majesty. You see, I chose your son for a specific reason. With him in charge, it would be very easy for you or me to control things through him. Not explicitly of course, but more through advice and suggestion. Horus is a strapping young war god with many great accolades of his own already, so your naysayers on the Council might be more accepting of him than you," Thoth explained.

"Hmm... A puppet king? That's a rather devious plan, Thoth. I'm impressed. But what is this new change of action you came up with?" Isis asked.

Thoth pulled the horses to a slow trot and set down the reins, turning to face Isis. He hadn't had much time to fully work out this plan, but he knew that Isis would prefer this idea better.

"I've had many years to get to know our many acquaintances on the council. I've learned the various little eccentricities of everyone from Huitzilopochtli to The Jade Emperor himself. And today, I saw a certain someone crack under the pressure of his own failures. Did you happen to notice Zeus' reaction to you bringing up the Heracles Accords?" Thoth began.

"You mean that stupid look he always has?" Isis asked.

Thoth was unamused by her attempt at comedy, so he continued, "Yes, well to the untrained eye, it may not seem like much, but I could see it for what it was: a crack in his otherwise flawless mask. I have reason to suspect that the great Lord Zeus has broken his own personal Accord."

"So, you think we should take this information to Buddha?" Isis asked.

"No, not exactly. I'm suggesting that we take this information and use it against him. He seems to like going for the lowest hanging fruit when he goes for his insults, and while I'd never suggest sinking to his level, I would suggest breaking the hand he's using," Thoth replied.

Isis' eyes lit up with recognition as a devious smile crossed her lips.

"You think we could punish him with this. My question is how, exactly?" Isis asked.

"Well, Buddha would most likely want some kind of evidence. I think it would be best if we found this new mystery child and use them for one of two purposes. The first and most obvious is that at the next council meeting, when Zeus decided to try and undermine you, we use the child as a proverbial slap in the face," Thoth began.

Thoth paused for a second to let Isis react. She nodded and motioned for him to continue.

"The second option is that we find this child and use them as leverage," Thoth finished.

"Leverage? For what, exactly?" Isis asked.

"Whatever we desire. Respect, sacrifices, a higher standing in the council, anything. Leverage against Zeus means leverage against one of the strongest pantheons. We could easily bring the Olympians to our beck and call with one simple action. We could finally use them to crush our enemies. Set would finally bow to you, Apophis would no longer be a threat to Ra, anyone who would rise up against us could be crushed with ease. You would finally have a seat at the right hand of Buddha himself," Thoth explained enthusiastically.

Isis' eyes sparked for a minute before she shook her head.

"No, not like this. I will reclaim our lost glory, but not like this. Ra built our pantheon on his back, and I will not tarnish the legacy he left for us," Isis replied.

Thoth shook his head and placed a hand on her shoulder.

"With all due respect, my lady, that legacy was already tarnished by both you and Ra himself," Thoth said.

Isis' hand went across his face before he could continue. Thoth staggered back for a second and caught himself. Isis' eyes were ablaze, shining a fierce blue that rivaled the sky itself.

"It would be wise for you to watch your tongue, Thoth, or less you might lose it," Isis snapped.

Thoth took a second to compose himself, as it would do him no good to become angry here. He readied his next few words and spoke with great caution.

"Forgive me for overstepping, my lady. I merely meant that in the eyes of our, ahem, 'allies', our legacy is already in ruins. I believe rather than trying to hold on to a messy legacy, we take a chance on trying to build a new legacy. One that is stronger than our predecessor, and will hold strong far into the future.

"We could become the next great pantheon, one that will lead a dynasty that could lead all the realms into a future of prosperity. The only thing standing in our way are the old, misogynistic, pigs that sit on the council. If we find leverage against Zeus, we can take down one of the obstacles. Odin will follow shortly after, and The Jade Emperor could easily be brought to a knee when faced with our strength. I think I can speak for both of us when I say that I'm more than tired of the way those doddering old fools have been running things. Don't you agree that the time has come for some new blood to take over the council?" Thoth spoke carefully so as not to incite another burst of Isis' rage.

He hoped she would agree to this. He tried to appeal to her more competitive side, but now he was appealing to her reasoning. This was the same reasoning that led her to make the decision to usurp Ra, the same reasoning that pushed her to try and hold her standing in the council when it was clear she wouldn't be able, and the same reasoning that drove her to becoming the incredible leader she was.

Under her, Egypt was flourishing. Women were able to have children with fewer chances of dying or complications, crops flourished, allowing for better trade with other countries, and the pharaohs who could trace their lineage back to her ruled with wisdom and justice. She was beloved in Egypt, by both people and gods alike.

Despite her outward appearance and attitude, Isis wanted to help people. The thought of being able to help all of the realms with their struggles would appeal to her on the level that only a mother could feel. Thoth was quiet for a few seconds as he watched Isis ponder his words.

"What if this plan of yours fails? What of our legacy then?" Isis asked.

Thoth felt a surge of triumph rise in his chest. His gamble paid off, but it could still easily fail if he wasn't careful.

"We use Set," Thoth said.

"WE DO WHAT?" Isis screamed.

Thoth knew this was a high-risk play. Set had been an enemy of the pantheon since he trapped Isis' husband, Osiris, in a sarcophagus and dismembered him.

"Please, allow me to explain," Thoth said.

"You had better make it quick, or you'll be guiding Ra's boat through the underworld for the rest of the millennia," Isis growled.

Thoth swallowed the lump in his throat, knowing both the danger of his potential punishment, and that Isis would happily follow through.

"I understand your trepidation, but hear me out. Set is a god of disorder and violence, if he somehow got a hold of this information, what do you think he'd do with it? This demigod could easily wind up in Set's possession, wherein we then send out a rescue mission for them. We make a display of strength over one of our enemies, and we rescue a new demigod. From there, we have two options; we can either hold on to the child and throw him in Zeus' face when he tries to push you, or we could return them and be rewarded with Zeus' debt," Thoth explained his plan with the deliberate determination of a man pleading his case before a hangman's noose.

"There are some very serious flaws in this plan of yours. For one thing, Set is not going to play along with any of this. Knowing him, he's going to immediately try to destroy the entire plan. He may even kill this little demigod. If he did that, Zeus would have grounds for a war. Is that what you want?" Isis asked.

"Of course not," Thoth replied quickly.

"And all of this is running off the idea that Zeus, ZEUS, would actually care enough about a child of his that isn't a hero! That man probably doesn't even know how many kids he has, and you expect him to give a damn about this mystery child, who may or may not even exist. Thoth, I appreciate your advice, but I feel like this plan of yours isn't your best work. Maybe you're right, maybe we should try to implement some sort of puppet monarchy with Horus." Isis sounded defeated as she looked out over the horizon.

Thoth felt defeated as well. He knew that this plan wasn't his best work, but it was the best chance their pantheon had to regain any semblance of respect. He was certain that this had to work, but Isis was right about the variables.

Set was a wild card, but he would also be the only god at their disposal that no one would expect them to work with, and while he wasn't certain that this mystery demigod existed, he had seen Zeus crack at the mention of the Heracles Accords. Thoth could make this work, he just needed time.

"My lady please, give me one year. In one year, I will bring you a plan with no variables, no possibility of war, and one that could guarantee respect," Thoth pleaded.

Isis shook her head and replied, "No. We can't take one year. A lot can happen in a year, and we don't want to risk pooling our resources somewhere else when something completely unprecedented is happening right now. Everyone's on edge dealing with this potential new threat. Our enemies could move now while we're distracted, and without your mind focused on the task at hand, they could take advantage and overrun us."

Thoth dropped to a knee and lowered his head before begging again, "My lady, please. If not one year, then give me six months. I vow that my mind will remain focused on the task at hand, and in my free time, I will focus on filling out this plan to your satisfaction."

"You won't let this go, will you?" Isis asked, rubbing her head.

"I'm afraid not," Thoth said, rising back to his feet.

Isis sighed in response before nodding.

"Thank you, my lady. I will not disappoint you," Thoth replied with a bow.

Chapter 14

"I feel like your plan has some holes in it," Zeus said as Athena steered the chariot.

"Yes, well, I wasn't really expecting Buddha to be blind to him as well. So I had to improvise a little bit," Athena replied.

They had been flying for a few minutes before either of them spoke. Athena's mind was racing with the many possibilities of what could happen in the coming weeks or months.

Would she be proven right, or would there be yet another unforeseen complication?

No one could've guessed that Buddha wouldn't be able to see this man. Hiding from a god is difficult, but doable in some very rare circumstances. Zeus had hidden from Hera many times, using a variety of different methods from storm clouds to extremely talkative nymphs.

To hide from a god was a feat on its own, but to hide from multiple gods was thought to be impossible. Then, to be able to hide from the Buddha as well, there was no doubt in Athena's mind that this man, whoever he was, had to be something special. Athena's mind was filled with so many questions and theories that she hadn't even fully started to process them. Zeus' random statement brought her back to reality.

"Isn't improvisation the enemy of wisdom?" Zeus asked.

"No, the enemy to wisdom is ignorance, Father. One would expect you to know that," Athena retorted.

"Your mouth seems to be running unfiltered today," Zeus rumbled.

"Forgive me, today put me on edge in a way I wasn't expecting. In truth, I knew this plan was going to be a long shot," Athena replied.

“Yes, well, let’s make sure we don’t lose our standing in the council. I’ve worked far too hard in the last few centuries to let all of that be washed away because you didn’t have an adequate plan for countering a mortal,” Zeus said.

“At ease, Father, I can assure you that we won’t lose any standing in the council. As for your comment about countering a mortal, I have a theory that whoever that man was, he wasn't mortal,” Athena explained.

Zeus’ eyebrow raised in response. Athena took the opportunity to expound on her point; “Do you remember Odin and Isis’ little magic show? Isis couldn’t locate him with her magic, and whatever Odin tried caused the entire spectral tree to become covered in that black energy and fall apart. Nothing, to my knowledge at least, has ever been able to avoid both Isis and Odin, and I’ve never seen tracking magic react like that to anything. I feel like there’s something more going on that we’re not privy to.”

Zeus groaned before replying, “Merciful Buddha, please don’t tell me that you’re buying into Odin’s Ragnarök nonsense.”

A millennia ago, when Odin hung himself from the branches of Yggdrasil, the tree blessed him with more magical secrets than any other god. As he hung for nine days and nine nights with his own spear embedded in his side, the tree filled his mind with knowledge of magic and runes, but Yggdrasil forced Odin’s psyche to pay in retribution.

The tree assaulted Odin’s mind with visions of great battles that tore through the realms. Gods, giants, monsters and demons clashed for what seemed like years as the realms burned and crumbled around them. The images were too fast and hazy for Odin to make out any definitive details, but the experience changed him.

He became more reserved, and started to covet knowledge and prophecies in an attempt to try and make sense of the visions.

The gods all knew that their time would come someday. Many assumed they would simply age and pass on the torch, just as their forefathers had done before them. But Ragnarök was different.

From what Odin described, it wasn't just the end of an era, it was the end of everything. Many didn't believe it was possible, and some, like Zeus, actively despised the entire idea. Athena figured that they wanted to live in blissful ignorance, simply pretending that the slew of enemies that lurked in the shadows were flaccid in their threats.

Each pantheon had enemies, and each pantheon had blood on their hands as well. Most were banished, imprisoned, or, in some cases, butchered beyond repair, but not every enemy was so easily swept under the rug. Athena had often wondered what would happen if they all converged into one single force, and she believed the answer to be Ragnarök. She believed that all they needed was a single unifying banner, a cause strong enough for them to fight and die for, and she hoped that they would never find it.

"Father, with all due respect, even you have to admit that something strange is going on. A mysterious man, whom no one in any of the realms, not even the Buddha himself, has ever seen, arrives on our doorstep. He nearly walks away with ambrosia before facing off against four Olympians, two of whom are war gods. Before leaving, he explodes our minds with pain, including the mind of the Earthshaker himself. He caught your lightning and threw it back at you, nearly taking your head off. Do you truly think that anything in all the realms would be capable of that if it wasn't some sort of sign that the end times were coming?" Athena explained.

"It was a fluke, nothing more," Zeus grumbled, resting his chin on his hand.

"A fluke? Father, when Ares beat Heracles in an arm wrestling contest, that was a fluke. This wasn't a fluke, this was something more," Athena replied.

"The reality of the situation is most likely more mundane than that."

"And what would that be?"

"My best guess? Some kind of coup, probably led by Isis, given her history. She probably used a mortal that wouldn't draw anyone's eye, cast some kind of overly complicated spell, and made all of this happen right under our noses. I would even hazard a guess that her and Odin might be working together, and their little magic display during the council was all an act meant to throw us off their scent. If it worked on you, then I have no doubt that it worked on some of the others. Unfortunately for Isis, however, I am much too smart for something so trivial."

Athena scoffed at her father's arrogance. She genuinely couldn't tell if he was being serious or not. A coup, even one led by two of the most powerful magicians in all the realms, would never work against Buddha. He saw everything and was the single most powerful being in the realms. Sun Wukong sat at his right hand, and no one would ever risk crossing him willingly. Zeus was letting his own frustrations blind him to the obvious truth of the situation.

"Father, think rationally. A coup against Buddha would accomplish what exactly?" Athena asked.

"Isis would use it to gain power, control, or whatever it is she wants," Zeus replied.

"But how would turning a mortal into a god result in any of that?"

"I don't know yet, but it makes more sense than believing everything is going to result in the end of the world."

"Yes, of course. I forgot that turning everything into a conspiracy of how every god in your general vicinity wants to overthrow you is much more sane than simply believing there's something you can't understand going on."

"I've had enough of your mouth today, young lady."

"You can get mad as much as you want, the realms do not revolve around you. That news might shock you, but it is in fact possible that this man has nothing to do with any pantheon and may be some sort of anomaly that could signal a larger problem. Maybe it's time to stop thinking everyone is out to overthrow you and start reaching out to some of the other pantheons and start forming real genuine alliances."

She turned to face her father and was met with a backhand across her face. Athena had seen it coming, she had been pushing her luck with Zeus all day. She took the slap without flinching, holding her head high as Zeus loomed over her.

"You will watch your tongue, or I will remove it. You are my advisor during the council meetings, but I don't need your assistance outside of it. I have led our pantheon for the last three millennia, through war and strife. We have prospered because of me, and me alone. You don't lead for three thousand years without learning to look over your shoulder." Zeus growled.

Athena turned back to the reins and didn't speak until they arrived back at Olympus.

Chapter 15

Odin stared over the horizon, tapping his fingers on the rim of the chariot. Tyr had waited for him to speak, but as the minutes began to drag on, he decided to break the silence.

"So... Can I ask about what happened back there with Isis' magic display?" Tyr asked.

Odin was quiet for a few seconds as he seemed to mull things over.

"I'm not sure myself, honestly. But I've been working on a few theories," Odin replied.

"I'm guessing your theories have something to do with Ragnarök?" Tyr asked.

"Well, partially. I don't doubt that this mystery mortal will have something to do with Ragnarok. If I had a name, I might be able to find out something. For now, though, my standing theory is that this mystery mortal might have the potential to be a god killer," Odin replied.

Tyr's eyes flicked to the stump at the end of his right wrist.

"Do you think that's possible?" he asked, his mouth running dry at the idea.

"I wouldn't doubt it. If this person is, we might need to try and imprison him the way we've done before," Odin replied.

Tyr thought back to the day they imprisoned Fenrir. Fenrir was the oldest son of Loki, and, like most of Loki's children, he was a monster. Fenrir's body took the form of a wolf, but it grew larger and larger each day.

Odin had brought him to Asgard when he was only three years old, and he was already the size of a stallion. Fenrir was the only child Odin had chosen to save, mostly because he believed that he could use the beast to strong-arm the other pantheons into following him. They kept the wolf for many centuries, long enough for Tyr to bond and develop a friendship with him.

Everything changed, though, when Odin hung himself from Yggdrasil. He wouldn't elaborate on why, but he began to try and bind Fenrir. He hid the attempts under the guise of testing Fenrir's strength, and Fenrir, being naive to the cruelty of the gods, leapt at the chance to prove himself to the Asgardians.

Each week for a century, Odin would come with thicker and stronger chains. Chains imbued with magic, chains made of the strongest materials in the realms, all fall victim to Fenrir's strength. Desperate, Odin went to the dwarves for help.

After three months, the dwarf king supplied Odin with three silk ribbons. The king explained that the ribbons were crafted using the strongest of ingredients, and would bind Fenrir completely, body and soul. Tyr accompanied Odin to visit Fenrir for this final trial. Fenrir had grown taller than even Mount Olympus itself, and could no longer live on Asgard, so the three would be completely alone.

To this day, no one on Asgard, not even Loki, knows what really happened. Odin's official story was that something went wrong with the binding spell and Fenrir was choked to death as a result. In this version, Tyr had tried to save his friend, but got his hand caught in the binding as it tightened.

The truth was arguably worse. Upon arrival, Fenrir was excited for another test of strength, but grew skeptical when Odin revealed the ribbons. Fenrir agreed, but only with the condition that someone would place a hand in his mouth as a sign of trust.

Tyr accepted and placed his right hand into Fenrir's mouth as Odin began to cast the spell. One ribbon wrapped around Fenrir's neck, the second bound his front legs together, and the third wrapped around his back legs. The three ribbons converged and wrapped around his chest, forming an unbreakable knot.

Fenrir tried for three days to break the ribbons, but was unsuccessful. He finally admitted defeat, and relaxed to allow Odin to release the ribbons. Odin refused, surprising Fenrir and sending him into a tirade of curses. Tyr had every chance to move, but he allowed Fenrir to take his hand as retribution for his betrayal.

Odin took the chance to draw a magic sword and drive it into Fenrir's maw. The sword extended and pierced into the ground, pinning Fenrir in place. Odin and Tyr left him there, but Tyr had taken a look back to see the tears from his former friend.

"You're not going to try and control him?" Tyr asked.

Odin shook his head and replied, "No. For all I know, Buddha has some kind of plan laid out for when they find him."

"I wouldn't doubt it. I'm sure we're not the only ones with a lot of questions after today. What's our plan moving forward?" Tyr asked.

"We wait it out for as long as it takes. Once I have a name for this mystery mortal, or immortal now I suppose, I'll be making a trip to Thoth's library to see what we can gather," Odin replied.

"Do you think Thoth will be willing to help you?"

"The Egyptians have just as much stake in this as we do. While Isis may not believe me about Ragnarök, Thoth has never questioned me. Besides, he's most likely come to the same conclusion I have."

"The conclusion about this man potentially being a god killer, or that he might have something to do with Ragnarök?"

The conclusion that there's only one way for us to know for sure, Odin thought before answering. "Both, most likely. Thoth is an intelligent man, I have no doubt that his mind works the way mine does. He's probably running through a thousand possibilities as we speak."

Tyr chuckled to himself.

“Something amusing you, Tyr?” Odin asked.

“Oh, nothing, I just forgot how close you and Thoth are, that’s all,” Tyr said with a smile.

Odin nodded in response. He and Thoth had been friends for the last fifteen hundred years. They had known each other for a few centuries before, but didn’t truly become friends until they discovered a shared love of knowledge, and riddles.

They began meeting up every year for a riddle contest, then more frequently for games of chess, and before they realized it, they had become the best of friends. When he was out wandering, Odin would frequently stop by Thoth’s library for a drink and chat, and Thoth was always accepted on Asgard. However, more than friendship bound them together. The two shared a secret. One that, if discovered, could ignite a war.

Chapter 16

The last two months had been a breeze for Tala. Thunder had taken her under his wing, taught her the ways of being a leader, and listened to her council when she supplied it. The village had truly come to respect her as a leader, and she had taken to it with gusto. They had successfully gotten the wall built around town, allowing for more people to help on the farms.

The additional sixty hands even allowed for some of the men to start construction on additional homes so not everyone would have to stay in the cramped mead hall. Tala had taken a few days to carve a barrier similar to her mother's around the wall, protecting it from the elements and any potential attacks. It took a few days for her to figure it out, but she was happy when she finally managed it.

It was the final day before Gaius was set to return, and Tala found herself sitting outside the hall, reading a scroll. Thunder was leading a hunting party, and left her in charge while they were gone. The sun shone overhead, and the weather felt beautiful as fall was close to setting in.

"Are you excited for tomorrow?" a voice asked.

Tala looked up to see Forest limping over, heavily favoring his cane. She quickly leapt to her feet and ran over, giving him a careful hug.

"Yeah, I can't wait. Once Gaius gets back tomorrow, we can start prepping for the wedding. Then, by this time next week, I'll be married and ready to help lead our village into the future. I'm so excited," she replied.

"So much has already changed, I bet Gaius won't even recognize this place. Come to think of it, after two months of getting to know himself, will we recognize him?" Forest said.

"Please, this is Gaius we're talking about. I've known him for years, there's nothing he can do that would surprise me. He'd have to be an entirely new person for me not to recognize him," Tala replied.

Forest shrugged in response, not entirely sure if she was correct, but not feeling like dwelling on it either. He followed her back to where she was reading, and sat in the chair next to her.

"So, how have you been feeling?" Tala asked.

"Well, as of right now, I've been a little stiff. Your uncle warned me that the winter and fall will bring some serious complications, mostly stiff muscles and joints. He says it seems like I'm going to be village-bound from now on. No more hunting or building, but I think I'm ultimately fine with that," Forest explained.

"I'm so—," Tala began.

"You seriously need to stop apologizing. What happened to all of us wasn't your fault, so stop beating yourself up about it," Forest interrupted.

"You're right, sorry," Tala said.

Forest nodded and leaned back in his chair. They sat in silence for a few minutes when they suddenly heard shouting in the direction of the gate.

"What's going on?" Forest asked in surprise.

"I don't know, but it sounds bad," Tala replied, jumping to her feet and heading towards the gate.

"Wait, your staff!" Forest called after her.

"No time, I'll improvise!" she called back.

"That's not a good idea!" she heard Forest yell as she picked up speed.

The gate came into view, and she could see a large group of warriors holding back a growing crowd. There was too much noise for Tala to make out what was happening.

"What's going on?!" she yelled as she approached the crowd.

"They won't let me in!" a voice shouted.

The voice struck a chord in Tala's soul.

"Let me through! Let me through!" she yelled, pushing her way through the crowd.

The crowd cleared in front of her to reveal a tired and worn out Gaius. Three guards were around him, each with an outstretched spear ready to stab him.

"By the gods..." Tala whispered.

Chapter 17

The last two months had been a living hell for Gaius, that much was clear just by looking at him. Dark circles shadowed his eyes from countless sleepless nights, their usual shine dulled by exhaustion. He had lost weight, and the clothes he wore were the same ones from the day he left. He managed a small smile for Tala before turning his attention back to the men around him.

"Who are you guys, anyway? I've never seen you around," Gaius asked.

"Stand down," Tala ordered.

"But—!" one guard began to protest.

"Stand. Down," Tala repeated, stepping forward.

The three guards lowered their spears and backed away. Tala threw her arms around Gaius, who seemed to almost collapse into her arms.

"By the gods, what happened to you? You look like shit," Tala asked, squeezing him tighter.

"It's a long story, needless to say I'm exhausted. It would sure be nice to get some sleep on a comfortable bed for the first time in two months," Gaius grumbled into her shoulder.

"Are you sure? It's only noon," Tala asked.

Gaius' body seemed to grow heavier as a response.

"Okay, come on. Let's get you to bed, I guess," Tala said, getting Gaius' arm around her shoulders.

It didn't take as much effort as the last time he leaned on her, but it still took a few minutes to get him to the hall. As they walked, Gaius seemed to drift in and out of consciousness, which made it hard to navigate the steps and get to Gaius' room.

"Keep... quiet... Birds... Ravens..." Gaius muttered as Tala opened the door.

"Huh?" Tala asked.

"Ravens... Sun... Eyes... Every—," Gaius muttered.

He stopped when he saw the bed and immediately collapsed onto his face.

"Gaius?" Tala asked.

Gaius didn't respond, and Tala figured he was asleep. She ruffled Gaius' hair, and noticed the small jug tied to his pants. Tala untied it and opened it, taking a sniff of it as she did. It smelt sweet, like a mead. Gaius wasn't known to be much of a drinker, she wondered if this was supposed to be a gift for her. She contemplated taking a sip, then thought better of it and set it on his nightstand before heading out of the room.

Gaius had spent the last two months on the run. He was constantly moving, hiding from the sun, the moon, any birds, insects or other animals that might cross his path. He had stopped eating as much as he needed to, slept only a couple hours each night, if that, and wasn't able to return to the city to get his clothes.

Thanks to his newfound immortality, he didn't starve to death, or die of dehydration. The only upside to it, at least in his mind, was that he was able to push his telekinesis beyond what he thought were his limits. He was stronger now, mentally at least, even though his body had deteriorated from lack of care.

Now that he was home, though, he was certain things were finally going to improve. After all, it's not like things could get any worse, right?

By the time he woke up, the sun was setting. The smell of food sent his stomach into a roaring frenzy. He pushed himself to his feet, and staggered to his door. The room spun around him and he nearly fell into the door. Despite just waking up, he was still exhausted.

Leaning against the door, he could hear Tala and Thunder talking down the hall.

"… Muttering about birds and eyes. It was weird," Tala said.

"Birds, huh? Maybe he ran afoul of some gods," Thunder replied.

"You think so?" Tala asked.

"Well, yeah, it probably wouldn't even be hard for him. With his attitude, and how ornery some of the gods can be, it's the perfect concoction for disaster," Thunder explained.

"You think it could be serious?" Tala asked.

"I doubt it, gods can hold grudges, but most only seek revenge if the crime was serious enough. He wouldn't have made it home if the gods truly wanted to find him," Thunder sounded nonchalant in his response. He would know, after all.

Gaius was reaching for the door handle when Tala asked a question that stopped him. "If it was serious, though, do you think we'd be in danger?"

"Honestly, yes. Gods are vengeful by nature, and everyone and everything around the target of their rage is in jeopardy of getting caught in it. But, like I said, if they wanted him found, he never would've made it home," Thunder's answer sent a shiver down Gaius' spine.

The last two months he had been so caught up in his panic he hadn't even considered the dangers he could be bringing home. Thunder was right, the gods would be furious if they found him. He loved his family, but the thought of bringing down the wrath of Olympus, at least, on to his small village was enough to make him reconsider his choices.

He began to think he never should've come home. Gaius was putting everyone's lives at risk, and he hated the thought of his family getting hurt. He could run, jump out the window and fly until he couldn't go any further. It was the only way that we could save them from any potential danger of having him around.

The idea wasn't without flaw, running without an explanation would hurt Tala, something he desperately didn't want to do, but he had no true alternative.

Gaius, now more steady on his feet, walked over to the window and opened it. Warm air rushed over him, blowing his hair backwards. The sun was nearing the horizon, creating a sky of beautiful orange and blue. He took a shaky breath and braced himself. His eyes blurred with tears as he prepared to fly away, then he heard the doorknob turn. He quickly wiped his eyes and turned to the door as it opened. Tala stood in the doorway, a smile swept across her face when she saw Gaius.

"Hey, you're awake. Are you hungry?" Tala asked.

"I..." Gaius couldn't fully find the words he needed to articulate what he wanted to say.

"You...?" Tala asked, tilting her head.

A thousand thoughts raced through Gaius' mind at once. He contemplated leaving. He thought about Tala's smile, about how dangerous the gods had been when he fought them, about the nights he and Tala spent talking for hours. He thought about the children in the village and the warmth of holding Tala in his arms. And then, suddenly, he realized the words he wanted to say.

He took a deep breath and finished his thought. "Tala, I love you."

A look of shock swept over Tala, which was then replaced by one of the biggest smiles Gaius had ever seen on her face. Her answer caused Gaius' chest to pound.

"I love you too. Come on, dinner's ready."

She turned and headed back down the hall, leaving Gaius to enjoy the rush of euphoria that swept through him. It was the first time he had said it, and it was the first time she had said it back. Knowing that someone loved you was one thing, but hearing them say it was a rush unlike anything in all the realms.

He stared at the empty door frame for a few more seconds before turning back to the window. The thought of running away still itched in the back of his mind. Objectively, he knew it was the right thing to do, but the thought made his heart ache.

He wanted Tala to be his everything, his whole world, and his whole life. The thought of spending the rest of eternity without her filled him with a pain he hadn't known to be possible. He would relive that fight on Olympus every day for a millennium and it wouldn't match up to the pain he felt at the thought of leaving Tala.

I... I can't leave. Shit.

He had to leave, though. He was a danger to the village. If the gods found him...

"I'll fight them off again and again and again. I will protect my village, my family, even if war comes to our front gate. I won on Olympus and I'll win again. If I'm wrong, then let the Buddha himself strike me down," Gaius proclaimed to the sky itself.

He waited for a second with bated breath to see if his challenge would be taken. He breathed a sigh of relief when it seemed that the Buddha would let this blasphemy go. Whether he was right or not was something that only time would be able to reveal, but he would stand by his resolve.

Using his immortality, he would hone his skills and battle any divine being that came his way. One day, with his powers and Tala's combined, they might be able to make the gods realize that they were not to be trifled with.

He decided to go get something to eat. While it wasn't truly necessary anymore, it would still help end the pain he was in. Plus, it was what normal people did. He slowly made his way down the hall, his balance still a little unsteady.

"I need some water," he grumbled as he reached the sitting room.

Thunder was there, and smiled when he saw Gaius.

"There he is! The man of the hour!" Thunder boomed happily.

Gaius gave him a weary smile in response, before rounding the corner into the kitchen. Tala was busy setting the table, so Gaius got himself a mug and reached the ice box. He poured a cup from the bottle of water he kept inside and quickly downed the entire mug. The cold water hurt going down, stinging Gaius' parched throat as it went.

Tala watched in quiet amusement as Gaius slowly emptied the jug with three mugs. Gaius went back for a fourth mug, and realized it was empty. He offered a pitiful look to Tala, who smirked as she crossed the kitchen to him. She took the mug and the jug, one in each hand, and flicked her wrists. Both immediately filled with crisp, clean water. Tala handed the mug to Gaius who smiled before immediately downing it.

"Sorry, I'm just so thirsty," Gaius panted.

Tala chuckled as she put the water jug back in the ice box. Thunder entered the kitchen and took a seat in the nook against the wall.

"So, any new happenings in the world beyond our wall?" he asked.

"Can I get a quick briefing on what's been going on around here first? Like why are there new guards, and what seemed to be cots in the mead hall?" Gaius countered, sitting across from Thunder in the nook.

Thunder and Tala offered him a quick explanation of the last two months, including the nuckelavee, River's death, and the arrival of the survivors from Three Rivers.

"Wow," Gaius said after the briefing, "You guys have had a pretty busy couple of months. It's terrible what happened to River, I'm gonna miss him."

"We all do," Thunder patted him on the shoulder.

"Well, come on, what have you been up to?" Tala asked, setting the table.

Gaius knew he was going to have to lie. There was no way he could tell them the truth, not right now, anyway.

"Well, I went to Falling Star Lake, and did some searching around. I found a ruined house that seemed to strike some kind of memory. I went inside and... it just seemed to be right. I remembered... my mom. She was calling my name. And I remembered it," Gaius spun his yarn as well as he could, hoping they would believe it.

Thunder and Tala leaned forward in a quiet anticipation.

"It's Gaius. Gaius Vinces," Gaius said with a slight smile.

"Interesting," Tala said.

"Yes, very," Thunder added.

Gaius stared blankly at them, confused by their reactions.

"Oh, I see. You don't know what it means. Both names are Latin in origin, Gaius means 'rejoice' and Vinces means 'conquer'. Your name would seem to be a phrase used for a leader," Thunder explained.

"Your mom probably wanted you to be a strong leader," Tala added.

This is your birthright... the ominous voice repeated in his mind.

I really doubt my mother had anything to do with this.

"Umm... yeah. Maybe that's it," Gaius replied, uncertainly.

"Anything else?" Thunder asked.

"I did some traveling. Hit up a couple of big cities, met some people," Gaius answered nonchalantly.

"They say anything interesting?" Tala asked, sitting down next to Gaius.

Gaius thought about it for a second and realized this would be the perfect chance to broach the topic of immortality. He could use this opportunity to gauge if Tala would be willing to join him for eternity.

He took a chance and said, "Well, I have heard a rumor that there's a new immortal running around."

Thunder nearly spat out his drink.

"A new immortal? Isn't that against the Wukong Accords?" Tala asked.

Thunder nodded as he coughed.

"An absolute defiance of an almost universally voted accord, no less. There's no way in the entirety of the realms that's true," Thunder sputtered as he finally cleared the liquid out of his throat.

"Well, allegedly, he stormed Olympus, fought a few of the gods, and made off with some ambrosia," Gaius explained.

"Bullshit," Thunder said.

"Absolutely," Tala added.

Gaius felt genuinely insulted by their immediate dismissal of his actions and switched to the defensive. "It could be possible. Some mortals are incredibly strong, they could go toe to toe with a god."

Thunder and Tala looked at each other and broke out into a fit of laughter. Gaius felt the heat rise in his face.

"Listen, son, no matter how strong a mortal man is, he is no match for a god. Even the weakest gods have to hold back when facing a human. Their bodies are naturally stronger than ours, their magic is much more potent than anything we could ever manifest, and on top of that, their divine states are monstrous. If a god wanted a mortal dead, there would be nothing to stop them," Thunder explained.

"But what about—," Gaius began.

"No, Gaius. There's no 'what about' this or 'what about' that. Let me explain it like this: You are incredibly strong. At your best, you can put my back to the wall. Even you wouldn't be able to put up a fight against a god that was going in for the kill. Do you understand?" Thunder explained.

Gaius nodded, knowing all too well the reality of Thunder's words. Though the bruises weren't there, he could vividly remember the pain from his bout on Olympus. He thought it would be wise to push forward, rather than dwell on his battle and near defeat.

"Whether it's true or not, it did get me thinking about immortality," Gaius said.

"You should stop that, now. It's outlawed for a reason, and you don't want to know what the consequences are for violating that accord," Thunder's words were filled with a hard edge that Gaius wasn't prepared for.

Both Gaius and Tala stared at him, waiting for him to continue. Thunder took a sip of his drink before obliging. "Oh, I don't actually know what punishment they would have for it, but I can simply imagine it wouldn't be fun."

"Well, despite the risks, wouldn't you want to be immortal if you had the chance?" Gaius asked.

The room was quiet for a minute while Thunder and Tala mauled the question over. Gaius felt his heart pound against his ribs in anticipation.

Tala spoke up first, "Despite how great it seems on the surface, being immortal would mean outliving all your friends and family, so it doesn't seem like it would be worth it."

"Yes, I'd have to agree. It doesn't seem as appealing when you really sit down and look at what it would entail," Thunder added.

Gaius was dumbstruck. He hadn't expected either of them to say no.

"But it would let you recover from combat almost instantly, you could push yourself further than you ever thought possible, you could—," he began.

"Not everyone likes to fight as much as you, Gaius," Thunder interrupted.

"I'd have to agree with that, while you might enjoy risking your life, it's not for everyone," Tala added, her grip on her mug tightening.

"But enough talk on this subject, we have a wedding that needs to be planned," Thunder chirped, clapping his hands together.

The two began to discuss details of the wedding, with Gaius only barely listening. He hadn't been ready to admit it, but he didn't expect her to say yes.

After all, she was right, Gaius would've been asking her to abandon everything she had known to be with him forever. It was the exact reason he had wanted her to become immortal with him. He would need to find another way to convince her, and he stewed on this for a few minutes until Thunder provided him with the perfect opportunity.

"I'll check with Grass tomorrow and see if we have any of the ceremonial wine ready or if we need to start prepping some," Thunder said.

"Actually, I have a mead upstairs I bought from a couple merchants I was hoping that we could use," Gaius piped up.

"A mead, huh? Why don't you pour us a glass so we can try it?" Thunder asked.

"No!" Gaius practically yelped in surprise.

Thunder and Tala stared at him in surprise and confusion.

"I— Um... I mean, I can't. I only have enough left for one goblet. I drank a lot of it on the way back, and wanted to save what was left for a special occasion," Gaius quickly explained, hoping his poker face would hide the lie.

"I didn't know you were much of a drinker, Gaius," Tala replied.

"Well, one of the cities I visited showed me that I actually do like alcohol," Gaius did his best to keep his face as straight as possible.

Tala looked to her father, who shrugged in response.

"The big cities have some fantastic drinks, it would be enough to change anyone's mind," Thunder said.

"Well, if that's the case, then we should use this magical mead for our wedding," Tala replied with a smile.

"Great, when are we gonna have the wedding?" Gaius asked.

"Well, we could have it next week. It would give everyone a chance to prepare, and give you enough time to rest," Thunder replied.

Gaius' chest swelled with pride and happiness as they continued planning the wedding, but he finished his food in silence. There was a nagging feeling in the back of his mind, his conscious telling him that this wasn't a good idea. He knew that he shouldn't lie to Tala, but she had made a choice.

I just hope she'll be able to forgive me one day. I can't say I'd blame her if she didn't.

He watched as her and Thunder spoke excitedly about the wedding, his chest growing heavy with guilt and regret.

Chapter 18

Gaius and Tala had had two very different weeks. For Tala, the week had been a rush of planning and prep work for her wedding. For Gaius, the guilt building in his chest was getting worse and worse with each passing day. The night before the wedding, he sat on his bed staring at the jug of ambrosia.

Should I do this? It's not too late to back out. I could 'accidentally' knock you over in my sleep and just settle for her spending her life with me. But what about after she's gone? Guess I have a few decades before that happens. Hopefully.

Gaius laid down and closed his eyes. In no time at all, he was asleep, and strangely enough, dreaming. He was on the shores of Falling Star Lake again, laying on the beach with his feet in the water.

Well, this is... new, I suppose.

"I thought you might want a break, given how stressful this past week has been," a familiar old voice said.

Gaius sat up to see the old woman he had meant two months ago in this same spot.

"You!" Gaius yelled, jumping to his feet.

"Hello again, you're looking... Tired," she said.

"Um... Yeah. I've had a rough week. Are you really here or am I dreaming?" Gaius asked.

"Yes, to both. I'm currently infiltrating your dream so that we can talk," the old woman explained.

Gaius blinked in surprise.

"It's probably better not to wrack your brain about it," the old woman said, sitting down.

"Just who are you, anyway?" Gaius asked.

"You don't need to worry about a name for me. Just know that I'm your ally, and that I know everything that's going to happen, and that has happened," the old woman replied.

"Does that include what I'm going to do tomorrow?" Gaius asked.

"Yes," the old woman motioned for him to sit down, which Gaius obliged after a moment of hesitation.

"Okay, then I have a follow up question. Do you think it's the right thing to do?" Gaius asked.

The old woman took a deep breath, seemingly gathering her thoughts before answering. "That's a difficult question to answer. On one hand, turning her immortal against her will isn't the best wedding present ever. But on the other hand, I... doubt you would reach as far as you do without her."

"Will she forgive me?"

"Not anytime soon, but someday she will. But you need to listen to me right now, this path that you've been on since I told you your destiny needs to end here. You can't keep pushing your will onto mortals because you think it's what gods should do. Times are changing. The realms will be changing soon as well. You're proof of this. You need to stop trying to be the god you think you should be, and become a god that embraces the greatest element of human nature."

Gaius listened intently, and waited for her to continue. She looked at him, and waited a few seconds for him to take the hint.

"Oh, it's my turn? Well, I'm guessing that the greatest element of human nature would be... Willpower?" Gaius asked.

The old woman shook her head. "No," she said. "The answer is love. Love for your family, your friends, fellow humans, your world, and yourself."

"I feel like there's a lot of options before love. What made you pick that one?" Gaius asked.

"You're right, there are more options before it, but love is more important than you realize. You're just too young to see it yet," the old woman replied.

"Just as cryptic as last time," Gaius muttered, pulling his legs to his chest.

They sat in silence for a minute until Gaius finally asked another question. "Am I destined to be a terrible person?"

The old woman leaned back on her hands and looked at the sky. An eternity seemed to pass before she answered. "No, not a terrible person, just a person. You'll make mistakes, some minor, some much worse than you realize, but that doesn't make you a terrible person."

"How can you say that after everything I've done? After what I'm about to do."

"Because you try to change and do better. Horrible people, the ones most people call monsters, they don't try to change. They lie, cheat, steal, kill, and they relish in it. They buy into the belief that they're incurable, or that they're perfect. They either don't see what they're doing is wrong, so they refuse to change, or they acknowledge that they're wrong, but refuse to change anyway. I've seen monsters before, of both kinds. They're stagnant and unchanging, despite the movement of the world around them. Change is the nature of all things, and those who fight it are doomed to fail. You will change, and that's what makes you better than them."

"I don't think I'm better than anyone."

"You haven't meant the monsters I have. You just have to learn to ignore that little voice in your head telling you to be a fool."

"When you say that, I'm assuming it isn't metaphorical."

The old woman's face hardened in a way Gaius wasn't expecting. "No," she said. "No, I'm not."

Gaius watched her quietly for a few seconds. Something about the way she set her face seemed to strike a chord in his mind. The way she clenched her jaw reminded him of someone, but he couldn't place a finger on it.

He cleared his throat before speaking again. "You know who it is, don't you?"

"Yes."

"And you can't tell me, can you?"

"I wish I could. There's a lot I wish I could tell you, but there's a good reason why I can't."

"Of course there is," Gaius' words dripped with sarcasm.

"Look, I know this is frustrating, believe me I know. But the reality is that right now, I simply need you to take these words to heart. That voice you keep hearing is not your friend. It does not want to help you. And you will need to watch your back. You're going to be facing a lot of trials in the coming future, and there are those who will try to lead you astray, those who will try to manipulate you for their own goals, and you need to be careful."

"And you can't tell me who those people are?"

The old woman took a deep breath and sighed. "Believe me, if I could help you, I would. But this is something you have to do on your own. To become who you have to be, who you are meant to be, you will need Tala and Ir—," the old woman stopped herself.

Gaius tilted his head in confusion. "Tala and who?"

The old woman pursed her lips, mulling over the question for a few moments. Then, her eyes suddenly lit up, and she said, "You haven't met him yet, but there's a young man named Iris who is going to play a crucial role in your life. He may not seem like much at first, but he'll become your best friend, like a brother to you, a real brother. He'll always be there to help you and Tala."

Gaius blinked in surprise. This was seemingly the first straight answer she had given him. But who was Iris? He had never meant anyone with a name that unusual before. This sparked his curiosity more than anything else the old woman had said all night.

"I probably shouldn't have told you that, but you should probably know about him before you meet him. If I sent you out there constantly looking over your shoulder, you probably would never trust him," the old woman explained, pulling Gaius out of his thoughts.

"Yeah, you're probably right. Thank you, I guess," Gaius replied.

The old woman rose to her feet and looked around. "Well, I hate to cut this short, but it's almost morning and I have other business to attend to," she said, walking up the beach.

"Wait, hang on! I still have questions! When will I see you again?" Gaius called after her, jumping to his feet.

"It won't be for a while, but you'll know when the time comes," the old woman said, continuing down the beach.

Gaius watched her walk for a few seconds before she stopped. Gaius perked up as she turned around. *Maybe she changed her mind. Maybe she'll answer some more of my questions.*

"By the way, do us both a favor and try not to beat yourself up too much. Like I said, you'll make mistakes, just try to learn from them," she said.

Gaius was about to respond, when he was suddenly awoken by a knock on his door.

"Umm... Yeah, come in," Gaius called groggily.

The door opened to reveal Thunder.

"Good morning, I was hoping you'd be awake already. Everyone's waiting downstairs to help you get ready," Thunder explained.

"Where's Tala?" Gaius asked, rubbing his eyes.

"She's getting ready with the help of the women of the village. Some of the men of the village agreed to help me get you ready, and we're all waiting for you downstairs. So hurry up and get dressed, we don't have all day," Thunder said, walking back down the hall.

Gaius stood up and walked to the window, the conversation he had with the old woman replaying in his mind. He wasn't truly sure if she was right, but he found himself hoping she was. He looked at the jug of ambrosia on his nightstand, and picked it up, removing the cork as he did so. The fruity smell filled his nose as he stared into the bottle and watched the golden liquid swish around. Gaius swallowed the lump in his throat and corked the jug, setting it back on his nightstand.

Whoever you are, I really hope you're right about all this.

The next few hours were a flurry of preparations and recitations that gave Gaius a bigger headache than the fight on Olympus. Thunder ran him through the traditional wedding vows of their people, while Forest and Wolf dressed him in clothes made of silk finer than any Gaius had ever seen in the village. When it was finally over, Gaius felt like an entirely different man.

"You clean up well, my friend," Forest said, clapping him on the shoulder.

Wolf nodded his approval with a huge smile. Gaius expected Thunder to say something. Before he did, Thunder headed to the kitchen and motioned for Gaius to follow him. Gaius turned to the others, who shrugged in response. Gaius took a deep breath and followed Thunder. Thunder stood in the kitchen with his hands behind his back.

"Everything okay?" Gaius asked.

"Yes. It's just that I have a present for you that I wanted to give you in private. It's something that my father gave me on my wedding day, which his father gave to him, and that I had hoped to give to my son on his wedding day. Fate seemed to have something different in mind, though, so I'm giving it to you," Thunder explained.

He pulled a small box from behind his back and opened it, revealing a necklace composed of three different colored threads, one red, one white, and one black. Hanging from it was a small dreamcatcher with three small, shrunken feathers dangling from it.

"It isn't much, but it's a family heirloom," Thunder said.

"No, it's great. Really. I can't believe you're giving it to me though," Gaius replied, staring at the necklace.

"Well, adopted or not, I raised you like a son, so it's only fitting," Thunder took the necklace from the box and draped it over Gaius' head.

Gaius' vision began to blur as he felt the tears swell. He cleared his throat and wiped his eyes.

"Thank you, really. It means a lot to me, and I hope I can make you proud," Gaius said.

"You already have. Seeing you grow into the man you are fills me with the same pride I get when I see the woman Tala's grown into," Thunder pulled Gaius into a hug and held him for a few seconds.

Sorry to disappoint you, old man.

Gaius pulled away and headed back into the living room with Thunder behind him.

"Well, we've only got a few hours. I'm going to go pay Tala a visit and check on her progress," Thunder said, clapping his hands.

He headed to the stairs, and left Gaius to talk with the other men.

"So, where's this mead we've heard so much about?" Grass asked.

"Yeah, bring it down and share it with your friends," Forest added.

"Um... I'd love to, but there's only enough for one goblet," Gaius replied.

The sound of boos filled the room.

"Ah, come on. Who only gets enough mead for one goblet?" one of the men asked.

"I drank most of it," Gaius didn't really think about how accurate that was.

"Yeah, good mead has a way of vanishing," someone said.

A murmur of agreement swept through the group, and from there, the conversation turned into a trading of stories about drunken escapades and conquests that Gaius chose to ignore. His mind wandered to Tala, and he wondered if she was as nervous as he was.

Probably not. After all, she's not about to ruin your *life because some mysterious old woman told you she'd eventually forgive you. You know, this is probably what she meant when she said about not beating yourself up so much.*

The remaining hours before the wedding quietly passed, and the weight in Gaius' chest grew heavier with each passing minute. When he got up to grab the ambrosia, each step took every ounce of strength and willpower that Gaius was able to muster. He crossed the room to the hallway which felt thousands of miles long, and practically had to force himself to move down it. The door seemed to fight to stay closed as Gaius opened it.

Gods, help me.

The bottle felt like it carried the weight of the ocean, but Gaius managed to bring himself to carry it downstairs. He was greeted by Thunder, who was practically bursting at the seams with excitement.

"It's about time. Come on, everyone's waiting," Thunder chirped, spinning on his heels.

"Yeah, I'm sure they are," Gaius muttered.

His feet seemed to refuse to move, and this caught Thunder's attention.

"What's the matter, son? Are you nervous?" Thunder asked.

“Um... No, I’m okay. I just... have some stuff on my mind,” Gaius replied.

“Anything you want to talk about?” Thunder asked.

“I’m just... worried about the future,” Gaius didn’t realize what he said until he heard them.

Thunder turned to face him with the look of a concerned father.

“What specifically are you worried about?” he asked with genuine concern.

Gaius knew he couldn’t tell him about Tala, so he chose to tell him about something else he had been thinking about for the last few days. “Well, to be honest, I’ve been wondering if I’ll actually be a good leader. I know you’ve been training Tala to be good, and I can lean on her, but what if that’s all I wind up doing?”

Thunder leaned against the wall and nodded. “I understand,” he said, “but you have nothing to worry about. Marriage is a two way street, with each person doing the best they can. Leaning on each other is just what you do.”

“Is that what it was like for you and Wind?” Gaius asked.

“Of course. She was my rock when I needed it, and I was hers,” Thunder replied.

Gaius smiled and started for the stairs, and Thunder followed. The mead hall had been totally transformed, with the long tables replaced by rows of benches. The throne on the platform had been removed and now an arch stood there with flowers growing around it. The entire village was seated on the benches and they applauded as Gaius stood at the bottom of the stairs.

Gaius looked at Thunder in confusion who merely motioned him forward. Gaius stepped forward and stood on the right side of the platform. Thunder took his place in the center of the platform, and raised a hand, motioning at the men at the door. They nodded and pulled the doors open, revealing Tala in a beautiful tan dress that hung down to her feet.

The dress was decorated in patterns of multiple swirling colors and shapes, not too dissimilar to her usual floral ensemble. Her long black hair was in a single neat braid that rested on her right shoulder. She wore sparse makeup, eyeshadow and some blush with red lipstick. Gaius felt his breath catch in his throat and his heart pound excitedly. Everyone rose to their feet as she walked down the aisle, and sat back down when she stepped on to the platform with Gaius.

"You look beautiful," Gaius whispered.

Tala replied with a smile that showed her teeth. Thunder cleared his throat and began the sermon.

"Welcome everyone, today we gathered to witness the union of Gaius Vinces and Tala. This union, if the great goddess Hera should deem it worthy, shall last a lifetime and bring them both happiness, love, and honor," Thunder began.

The whole service lasted for roughly thirty minutes. Thunder went through the entire service and walked Gaius and Tala through their vows. The time finally arrived for the ceremonial drink to bond the husband and wife as one. Gaius watched Thunder pour the ambrosia with a heavy heart that seemed to slow its beating. The golden liquid filled the cup and Thunder raised it to the village in the crowd.

"And now, with this drink, we will join these two in marriage, and send them down the path that will lead to a long and happy life together," Thunder explained.

He handed the cup to Tala and continued to speak his sermon, but Gaius couldn't hear him over the sound of his heart pounding in his ears. After a few seconds, Thunder gestured for Tala to drink. She raised the cup to her lips and took a sip.

In the matter of a single second, many different things happened. A shimmer of golden light radiated across Tala's body, the ceiling to the hall seemed to collapse, and Gaius saw a flash of red before his entire body exploded in pain as his ribs and sternum broke to pieces, his skull cracked and his spine was broken to pieces.

Gaius' ears were ringing but he could still hear people's screams and yells. He tried to move but his body was too broken to respond. His vision was blurry, but he could vaguely make out the golden outline of a head and the red eyes gleaming down at him. In what felt like an eternity, but was probably only a second or two, the ringing in his ears finally cleared as his skull shifted and fixed itself. He could hear Thunder's voice cutting through the static.

"Great Sage, please, what is the meaning of this?" he was asking.

"Sit down, little one, this is the official business of the Council. This young man here is a criminal who violated the Wukong Accords," Sun Wukong replied.

"I... What?" Thunder was flabbergasted.

"Yes. Apparently, he stole some ambrosia from Olympus and used it to become immortal," a new voice said.

"Stolen... Ambrosia?" Thunder asked.

"Dad?" Tala's voice asked.

"Everyone, please stay calm, there is no need to worry," a second new voice announced.

Everyone fell silent, and Gaius tried to move his head to see what was going on.

"Ah, this must be our culprit here. Victorious Buddha, if you'd please," the second new voice said.

Sun reached down and grabbed Gaius by his hair and lifted him up. The entire village was pressed against the wall, keeping as much space as possible from the four gods that were now in the room. Thunder was standing only a few feet away, holding Tala in his arms. Buddha, Zeus, and Odin stood under a gaping hole that was now opened in the ceiling. The Buddha walked forward with a smile.

“Well, hello there, young man. What’s your name?” Buddha asked.

Gaius opened his mouth to speak, but all that came out was a gush of blood and a gurgling sound.

“My word, what did you do to him?” Buddha asked Sun.

“I just punched him in the chest and stopped him from hitting the wall, by slamming him headfirst into the ground,” Sun explained.

That explains a lot. Gaius thought, taking a quick mental scan of his injuries.

The Buddha sighed and touched a finger to Gaius’ head. Gaius felt his body shift in uncomfortable ways and the bones and organs instantly healed and shifted. He sucked in a deep breath and felt a moment of joy, before the dread of the situation set back in.

“My name is Gaius Vinces,” he said, fighting his voice from his throat.

Odin’s eye narrowed on him as he spoke, and Zeus’ face hardened into a fury that froze Gaius’ blood in his veins. The Buddha offered a kind smile that did nothing to lessen the tension in the air.

“Well now, Mr. Vinces, would you care to explain your actions and why you willingly chose to violate an Accord?” the Buddha asked.

Gaius swallowed, acutely aware that every pair of eyes in the room was on him. But the two that cut the deepest belonged to Tala and Thunder. Tala looked confused, but Gaius could see the realization click to life in Thunder’s eyes. His eyes flicked from Gaius, to the cup, and then to Tala, then his eyes hardened with anger. The look pierced through Gaius’ heart like a red-hot knife and sapped any fight that remained from his soul. He dropped his gaze, unable to speak for several long seconds.

“You’d better answer,” Sun said. “Before old Monkey decides to stop you from hitting another wall.”

Gaius took a deep breath before speaking, “A few months ago, I met an old woman who told me that it was my destiny to become a god. So, I went to Olympus and stole some ambrosia. But, I couldn’t bring myself to drink the entire thing. I only drank half, and I... gave the other half to Tala.”

There was an uncomfortable silence for a few seconds.

“You... bastard,” Tala’s voice was low, but it resonated across the entire hall.

Gaius forced himself to look over at her, and he could see the tears in her eyes.

“I told you I didn’t want to be an immortal. I told you I was fine being just a mortal, but you... You took it upon yourself to force me into it,” Tala stormed across the room, her magic flaring to life around her like a raging inferno.

Odin seemed to take notice, watching her intently with his eye. She brought her hand across Gaius’ face in a vicious slap. The slap exploded on impact, scorching the side of Gaius’ face. He didn’t flinch, he took it without a word. Tala reared back for another slap, but her hand was caught by the Buddha.

“Now, now, let’s all just take a deep breath. This is an easy problem to solve. You haven’t willingly broken any Accords, so we can simply remove your immortality and you will suffer no consequence. You, on the other hand...” The Buddha stepped between Tala and Gaius. "...Are an interesting case.”

Gaius was confused as the Buddha stared at him for a second while he tapped his chin.

“Mr. Vinces, I can’t see you,” the Buddha said.

Gaius said nothing, but the look of confusion on his face deepened, as did the sense of confusion and unease in the room.

Buddha continued, "You see, I have the entire universe in the palm of my hand. I see everyone and everything, at all times, past, present and future. I see everyone in this room, and every ant in the ant hill outside, but for some reason, I can't see you. Odin had a similar problem with his ravens, Isis, with her magic, and Artemis with her hunting capabilities. You seem to be an anomaly of some kind, invisible to all who would try to find you."

As the Buddha spoke, Gaius felt realization come to light in his mind.

Those... "Entities" the old woman was talking about... If they have a stake in this then they must want to keep me unseen. She said they were more than gods, whatever that means. They have to have some kind of power to hide me from prying eyes.

"However," the Buddha continued, snapping Gaius back to attention, "we simply can't have you running around as a walking violation of the Accords. They are in place to protect mortals as much as they protect the gods, and allowing you to keep your immortality and continue to live as an immortal wouldn't be a smart choice on our part. So, we'll be needing to remove it."

Gaius didn't try to fight, didn't try to squirm, he knew he was outmatched. The Buddha could stop him in an instant, or Sun Wukong would easily break him again. There was no use in fighting, this was the end.

The Buddha reached out a hand to touch Gaius' head. Gaius closed his eyes, just as the Buddha and Sun yelped in surprise. Before he could open his eyes, he felt himself hit his knees. Gaius opened his eyes to see everyone staring at him, but something was wrong. He saw the world in a bizarre shading of black and grays. He looked around in confusion, before checking himself and seeing he was covered in a raging black fire. He screamed in surprise and threw himself to the floor, before remembering it couldn't possibly kill him. And, more curiously, it wasn't burning him or his clothes.

"What? What is happening to me?!" Gaius yelled as he got to his feet.

No one answered, merely staring on with looks of terror and shock. Even the mighty Sun Wukong himself was staring at his hand with a look of confusion and concern. Then, just as quickly as it started, the fire immediately stopped, leaving Gaius to blink as his eyes readjusted to the sudden flood of colors. The Buddha stepped forward and stared at him with intense curiosity.

"Well, that was... unexpected, to say the least," The Buddha seemed to be fighting a slight edge out of his voice. "And I'm guessing that you also don't know what that was either?"

Gaius shook his head, unable to find words that matched his disorientation. The Buddha looked from him to Tala.

"Ms. Tala, if you'd please," Buddha motioned her forward.

Tala took a few paces forward, and bowed. The Buddha reached out to touch her head, and her body erupted into black fire as well. She cried out in fear and began to smack at her arms, trying to put out the flames. After a second or two, the flames ceased to exist on her as well, leaving her with no signs of damage.

"Well, that settles it then," the Buddha said, clapping his hands together.

No one spoke, but all eyes turned to him.

"It seems that taking away your immortality might be out of the picture," Buddha announced.

"What?!" Tala yelled.

"Believe me, I understand that this is not what you want to hear, but there seems to be something more going on here. Victorious Buddha, if you'd please," Buddha explained.

Sun suddenly appeared at Buddha's side and held up the hand that he was using to hold Gaius a few moments before. Gaius' eyes grew wide with shock as he stared at the burn scars that covered it. Tala's jaw fell open as she looked from Gaius to Sun's hand.

"An immortal's body is capable of regenerating with no damage as long as the soul is still intact. Being able to leave a scar shows that the soul was damaged and had to restore itself, and if the soul is completely destroyed, the body will die as well. Whatever that fire was just now was able to damage the soul of not just an immortal being, but a Buddha no less. For now, until we can figure out just what is going on with you, you'll get to keep your ill-gained immortality. However..." The Buddha raised a hand summoned forth two golden rings. "We will need to keep the two of you under close supervision. You two will have to wear these rings, and they will bind you together. Wearing these two rings will keep you two from moving a maximum of one hundred feet away from each other. I am sorry about this, but the best way for us to watch you, is for us to watch her."

Tala's eyes simply seemed hollow as the Buddha placed the ring on her finger. She stared blankly at the floor as the Buddha placed the other ring on Gaius' finger. A spectral golden chain shot from the ring on Gaius's finger to the one on Tala's hand it hovered for a second before fading away.

"They won't come off without my permission, so don't waste your energy trying," the Buddha explained.

"So, what are we supposed to do, then?" Gaius asked.

The Buddha shrugged before turning to Odin and Zeus. "Do either of you have any ideas?"

Zeus said nothing, simply crossing his arms with a look of pure irritation. Odin scratched his beard before speaking. "The Underworld has records of all mortals, living and dead. That might be the best place to start."

"Ah!" Buddha replied with a smile. "Of course. That would be the perfect place to start this investigation. Victorious Buddha, would you mind giving these two a quick ride to the Underworld? The sooner we learn what's going on the better."

Sun crossed his arms and looked at Buddha with a sneer. "Old Monkey had to travel fourteen years on foot, while fighting various demons, how fair would it be to give them a shortcut?"

"You refuse, then?" Buddha asked.

Sun nodded his affirmation and stuck his tongue out. Buddha sighed before turning to Gaius. "My apologies, but it seems like you have a long trek ahead of you."

"I'm not going." Tala's voice was barely audible, but it pulled every eye in the hall to her.

"Tala—," Thunder began, before being stopped by Buddha's hand.

The Buddha placed a hand on her shoulder, causing Tala to look up with tears in her eyes.

"Come child," Buddha said, "Let us talk in private."

He led her outside with the gentleness and tenderness of a parent comforting a crying child.

"I understand your sadness and anger, but you must understand that we have no other options. If we cannot track him, we need your help," Buddha explained.

"I don't care, none of this is my fault and I'm being punished for it. I shouldn't have to be responsible for his actions," Tala protested.

"I know, and believe me, I wish there was another way. You must understand, though, that you're not being punished for his actions," Buddha replied.

"It sure feels that way."

"I know, and I'm sorry for that. Like I said, if we had another path, we would happily take it. This situation is unprecedented, and we have many questions that need answers. And in order for us to do that, we'll need your help."

"Find someone else. I won't forgive him and I won't travel with him either."

"No one ever said you had to forgive him."

"Huh?"

"Forgiveness is not something that should simply be handed out because someone asked for it. Forgiveness should be earned, but it's also wise to acknowledge when someone doesn't deserve it. And from what we've seen today, and what happened on Olympus, Gaius has a long way to go before he is worthy of forgiveness. Of course, whether or not you choose to forgive him is entirely your own choice, so you can choose not to even give him the offer of an olive branch."

"Wait, I don't understand. What are you saying?"

"I'm simply saying that should Gaius run afoul with another god, or even struggle with a monster or demon of some kind, it would be up to you if you choose to help him, or watch him struggle."

Tala was shocked, she would've never guessed that the Buddha himself would be so vindictive.

"You look surprised, little one. Did you forget that I was human once too? Enlightenment doesn't mean we forget the struggles of those who still climb the mountain," Buddha explained with a smirk.

"Isn't being petty like that counterintuitive to becoming enlightened?"

"We all reach our enlightenment in different ways. Learning the truth of one's life is a path that is different for everyone, I am not the way. Perhaps this is a chance to find your own way, and maybe giving Gaius his comeuppance is a part of that path."

The Buddha's words resonated deep in Tala's soul. He was right, she did need to find her own path. And despite how much she wished it wasn't true, her path right now seemed to be at Gaius' side. But the Buddha had been right about another thing as well, Gaius wasn't worthy of her forgiveness.

Not yet, at least.

Plus, it would be fun for her to watch him run afoul with the wrong god or monster. More than that though, Tala had questions about that black fire. She had never seen anything like it before, or even read of anything similar in her studies. It, much like everything else going on, seemed to be an anomaly with no obvious explanation or solution.

"All right, I'll go. But not for him, and not for you. I'm going because I want to figure out what's going on just as bad as the rest of you, and figure out how to get rid of this curse," Tala declared.

"That's fine. You should do it for your own reasons anyway, it's truly the only acceptable reason," the Buddha replied.

The two headed back into the hall, where very little of the scene had changed. Gaius now sat with his legs crossed on the floor, and Thunder sat on the stairs with his arms crossed and a deep scowl etched into his face. The air seemed to crackle with unspoken tension as Tala crossed the floor to her father. Thunder looked up, and Tala had never seen her father so sad. Even when her mother had died, her father stayed strong for her, but here, his eyes watered and she could tell this was killing him.

"I knew you'd have to leave one day, but I never would've guessed it would be like this," Thunder said, rising to his feet.

Tala threw her arms around him and they held each other for a few seconds, both of them fighting off tears.

"Be strong," Thunder whispered, kissing Tala on the top of her head.

"I was gonna tell you the same thing," Tala replied, squeezing her father tighter.

Gaius couldn't bring himself to watch as the weight of what he'd done crushed his heart. Instead, he turned to the gods in the room, and met the icy-blue eye of Odin straight on, sending chills through his body. He suppressed a shiver, and tried to stand straight as the god's eye moved around his body.

He's sizing me up. He probably thinks I'm a threat too.

Zeus, on the other hand, seemed to be more intently focused on Tala and Thunder. Gaius was curious what he was thinking, and contemplated reaching out his mind, then thought better of it and looked to the Buddhas instead. Sun Wukong had sat down, and was investigating his hands and their newfound scars. The Buddha himself, however, was watching Gaius. His expression was neutral and hard to read, but Gaius didn't feel any malice behind it.

He's probably waiting to see if I pull any more tricks out of the blue. I bet they think I'm responsible for whatever that fire was. What was that anyway? Just another mystery to add to the list I guess...

Movement caught Gaius' attention, and he turned to see Tala walking to stand before the Buddha. She bowed to him and he responded in kind.

"You'd best get on your way. The path to the World Tree is long and arduous, and I cannot see your futures, I can imagine it will be a rough journey," the Buddha explained.

"Yes of course, I merely need to go grab my staff, and then we can set out," Tala replied.

Chapter 19

Thoth's library was concealed within a never-ending sandstorm, navigable only by those who had his permission. Odin galloped through the swirling sands atop Sleipnir, the steed's eight legs effortlessly cutting through the relentless storm. The events of earlier that day played on a steady loop in his mind, and he found himself repeatedly turning over the two names he had learned.

Gaius Vinces... Tala...

The sandstorm began to thin and Odin arrived in the courtyard of the massive library. The courtyard was surprisingly green, with bushes and grass contrasting the raging sandstorm walls surrounding it. A large fountain sat in the middle of the walkway. The building itself was a huge temple that towered into the sky. It consisted of stone blocks, some of which were the size of a small horse.

Odin slid off of Sleipnir and tied him to a nearby pillar before approaching the massive set of oak doors. He raised a hand to knock, but the doors opened on their own to reveal the inside of the massive library.

From the entrance, Odin could see nothing but walls and walls of scrolls and books. Floating lanterns hovered around and bounced off shelves and walls. Thoth stood in the entrance, a floating book and quill hovering above his shoulder as he flipped through another book in his hands.

"Ah, hello. I've been waiting for you," Thoth said, not looking up.

"I assume you know why I'm here," Odin replied as the library doors closed behind him.

"Yes, a little birdy came by my window and told me all about your wedding crashing escapades," Thoth replied with a slight smirk.

"Horus, then?"

"Yes, Lady Isis was visited by Sun Wukong, who politely filled us in on the events of today. So, shall we then?" Thoth turned and headed deeper into the library.

Odin followed him, and they arrived in the center after a few minutes. The center was a thirty foot circular clearing with three desks and a long stone bench. The area was lit with sunlight from the massive skylight that was twenty stories above them. From this area, you could see the twenty floors above you, each one lined with a railing and with the same floating lanterns hovering around.

Odin followed Thoth past the library's center and deeper still into its labyrinthine corridors. After roughly ten minutes of walking, they arrived at the very end, a towering wall of scrolls. Thoth hummed a tune as he scanned the shelves before selecting a small scroll. In response, the entire wall trembled, and a section recessed before swinging open like a door, revealing a hidden chamber beyond.

It was dark inside, so he and Odin stepped inside and the door closed behind them, causing the torches on the wall to ignite.

In the center of the room was the secret that he and Thoth had to keep secret from the other gods. It was a man. He was tall, coming up to Odin's chest despite being chained to the floor. His red hair was dirty, long and matted, covering his face. His ribs showed through his skin. The man looked up, revealing bright red eyes that seemed to look past the two gods before him.

"Hello, Odin. I've been wondering when I'd see you again. Has the Buddha finally ordered you to free me?" the man asked in a hoarse voice.

"No, Prometheus, the Buddha still holds to his vow to not involve himself in the matters of the realms unless it is a matter of dire importance," Odin grumbled.

"Then what brings you to my humble abode?" Prometheus asked with a humorless chuckle.

"I've got names, and I need you to tell me what information you can about their future," Odin replied.

Prometheus looked to the ceiling and sighed. "No one ever just comes to visit," he grumbled. "Fine then, ask away."

"Gaius Vinces." Odin wanted to get the anomaly out of the way first. The odds were against Prometheus since even the Buddha couldn't see Gaius, but he wanted to exhaust all of his options before planning his next move.

Prometheus' eyes began to burn with an intense red light. "I see... I see... Nothing," he said after a few seconds.

Odin had expected as much, so he didn't dwell on it. Instead, he continued, "The next one is Tala."

Once again, Prometheus' eyes burned with the same red light. "She is fated to die next year."

Thoth and Odin quickly looked at each other, a single thought passing between them. *That's not possible.*

"You seem confused. Is there something wrong?" Prometheus asked.

Odin knew better than to answer that truthfully. Prometheus, while a valuable asset, was not one to trust. It was a lesson Odin had learned while the Titan was employed under Zeus and the Olympians.

Throughout his tenure as Zeus' advisor, he had tricked the god several times. Prometheus had tricked Zeus and bound the Olympians to accept lesser sacrifices on behalf of the humans. While this had greatly upset Zeus, it was not his most damning display of defiance.

Prometheus had stolen the spirit of fire from Olympus and hid it in a reed, granting it to the humans as present. This enraged Zeus, who beat Prometheus to within an inch of his life, and chained him to the tip of a mountain.

Zeus wasn't satisfied with this punishment, so he sent an eagle to rip open Prometheus' stomach each day and feast on his liver. Prometheus endured this for two centuries, living in a constant state of pain and suffering, until one day, Heracles had stumbled across him on his travels.

The Titan knew his coming fate, as he embodied foresight itself, and begged the demigod to kill him. Heracles refused, instead choosing to free Prometheus and continue on his way. Once Heracles was gone from sight, Odin's spear impaled him and stuck him to the ground. He was too weak to fight back, so Odin was able to bring him to Thoth's library, where they chained him to the ground and starved him for information.

He was Odin's eye to the future, a fact that the two gods were more than happy to remind him of any time he disobeyed.

"You're asking too much. Cease now," Thoth snapped.

"Come on, we have much to discuss," Odin said.

He and Thoth turned to the door before Prometheus' raspy voice raised up behind them, "Wait."

"We're done here," Odin replied, reaching out to the door.

"I saw something last night," Prometheus tried to raise his voice, but it wouldn't go above a dry wheeze.

Odin and Thoth looked at each other before turning around to face the Titan. "Speak then, and make it quick," Odin rumbled.

Prometheus lowered his head, and a smile stretched across his face. He kept it hidden and kept his voice leveled.

"It was Valhalla," Prometheus said.

Thoth looked at Odin, who clenched a fist with enough strength to whiten his knuckles. Valhalla was the realm that held Odin's army. He would take the souls of noble warriors who died in battle and bring them there, letting them eat, train and enjoy themself to their heart's content.

All the while, Odin's forces would grow stronger and stronger. He kept the army as a last resort option, something he could use to strongarm his enemies if they didn't cave to his will. For Odin, it was his pride and joy, he looked at it the way dedicated collectors would look at their toys.

"What about it?" Odin growled.

"It was on fire. Someone was burning it to the ground," Prometheus tried to keep the laugh out of his voice, but failed.

He didn't have the time to look up before Odin's fist came crashing down into his face. The entire library shook from the impact and golden blood sprayed across the wall as Prometheus' face hit the ground with a splat. Prometheus went to rise, only for Odin's boot to hit him in the chest.

Bones broke and Prometheus gasped as he slid back and slammed into the wall. Odin rushed forward to continue his beating, but was stopped by Thoth, who summoned a giant spectral hand to slam Odin into the wall opposite Prometheus.

"That's enough, Odin. He's just trying to get under your skin," Thoth said as he released Odin.

Odin's eye was locked onto Prometheus with a look of primal fury. Prometheus' body spasmed on the ground as he stared up at his captors.

"If you ever think you're going to touch what's mine, I'll make the last three centuries look like a night with Aphrodite," Odin growled.

He and Thoth left the room, with Thoth taking one last look at the broken Titan one final time before the door swung shut behind them. In the darkness, Prometheus chuckled to himself.

"Soon..." he whispered, "Soon, everything will come to light. Ragnarök is coming, Odin, and with it, your death."

Odin paced back and forth as Thoth wrote down their interaction on a scroll.

"That bastard... He thinks he is going to burn Valhalla... I'll drive Gungnir through his throat... I'll make him suffer... I'll..." Odin ranted as he paced.

"That's enough," Thoth stated, rolling up the scroll.

Odin looked at him, fury etched into the old god's face. Thoth kept his voice level as he spoke, trying to calm Odin down. "Those chains are unbreakable, magically connected to the roots of the Mountains of the Moon. There is no way a god, even if he is a Titan, could possibly break them without help. The only people that know he's here are you, myself and the Buddha. He's never going to escape, and no one is going to burn Valhalla."

Odin took a deep breath and calmed himself down. "You're right," he said. "I guess I just caught up in the moment."

You old fool, Thoth thought. *So concerned with the obvious threats, you lose sight of those moving in the shadows.*

"Say, while you're here, I was hoping you'd like to play some chess," Thoth said, gesturing to a nearby table.

"Actually, that sounds like fun," Odin replied, sitting down.

Thoth sat across from him as sand swirled around the tabletop, forming the game for them.

"Say, have your ravens heard any good gossip lately?"

Chapter 20

Tala walked ahead of Gaius by a couple dozen feet. He hadn't spoken to her since the wedding, choosing to let her have some space rather than attempt to explain his choice and make things worse. They had left the village a few hours ago, and dusk was starting to set in. The Buddha had pointed them north, and told them that they would need to scale the World Tree itself and brave its dangers to reach the Underworld.

"Hey, maybe we should—," Gaius began.

Tala turned around, her face etched with anger, just in time to see a spear fly down from the sky and stab through Gaius' back, pinning him to the ground. Tala went to step forward, then thought better of it, and stayed where she was. Gaius blinked in pain, unable to find his breath as the spear had struck one of his lungs. The sound of hooves filled the air around them, causing Gaius to crane his neck to try and look behind him. Tala gripped her staff and walked forward as Odin emerged from the forest on the back of Sleipnir.

"You should be smarter about who you give your identity to in the future, you never know how they might use it," Odin said, ripping his spear from Gaius.

Gaius collapsed to the ground and struggled to breathe. Odin got down from Slepnir and patted the stallion's back. Gaius flipped over and stared up at the god who loomed over him.

"Focus on your chest. Concentrate on the wound and it'll heal itself faster," Odin explained.

Gaius looked at him in confusion, then up at Tala, who had stopped a few feet away.

"Come on, I don't have all day. I'm not here to fight, or punish you. You have no reason to distrust me," Odin said.

Gaius couldn't believe that, but he had no other options, so he took the advice. He focused on the wound, and felt it almost immediately begin to heal. It only took a few seconds, and Gaius was able to gasp in a breath.

"I... Um... Thank you, I guess," Gaius gasped.

Odin didn't respond at first, merely watching Gaius as he brought himself back to his feet. Gaius was uncomfortable under the single blue eye of the All-Father.

"Is... Is there something you'd like to discuss?" Gaius asked as politely as his nerves would allow.

He had to keep his pride in check, for Odin was not one to be trifled with.

"Yes, there is, actually. You see, I realize the danger that a person with your... unique situation could cause if left to run unchecked," Odin began.

"I'm not unchecked though," Gaius interrupted.

"Yes, but a hundred feet is a large distance. Large enough for Mrs. Vinces—," Odin replied.

"Tala is fine." Odin looked over to Tala, who stared at him with crossed arms. "Or you can use the full translation, 'Stalking Wolf'."

Gaius stared at her, his jaw slack with shock. It wasn't her refusal to take his name that shocked him though, it was the attitude with which she spoke to Odin that caught him completely off guard. Odin's eye stared at her, boring into her soul, before suddenly softening.

He nodded to her. "My apologies, Ms. Tala. Back to my original point, a hundred feet is a substantial enough distance for you to hide a lot of actions, with or without her knowledge."

"So, you're going to mark me somehow as well?"

"No, I have no need to mark you with magic. As I'm sure you've figured out by now, I merely need to speak your name for Gungnir to be able to strike you into place. I don't need to mark you, or track you. Instead, I came here to secure you."

"Secure me?"

"Well, to be completely honest, I want to secure both of you."

"Both of us? Why?" Tala asked.

"Because I need strong allies who won't betray me. Tensions have been high between the pantheons for centuries, but the last few decades have brought many things to the forefront. Isis is now planning to try and dominate the Olympians by exposing Zeus' infidelities, giants of all races have been stirring restlessly, and the enemies of the gods have begun to move in the shadows. I fear that war is on the horizon, and I need to know which side you'll be fighting on," Odin explained.

"How do you know any of this?" Gaius asked.

"Huginn and Muninn, the ravens who watch everything." Tala answered, pointing at a tree to Odin's left.

A raven on a branch squawked in response, drawing Gaius' eye as it stared down at him.

"Very good, little magician," Odin replied with a nod. "You have great knowledge, and greater potential. Yes, my ravens watch all things in the realms, except for you of course. They see everything, whether it hides in shadows or dances in light. That's why I need to know that I can trust you, that the one being in all the realms that I can't see would be willing to aid me. Together, you and I can prevent any potential war from starting. We can deal with the enemies of the gods in secret, and crush resistance where it would rise."

Gaius looked from Odin to Tala, who still seemed to ignore him, but he could see her mind running from here. Gaius looked to Odin again, and immediately felt uneasy. Something in the back of his mind began to itch. For some reason he couldn't quite place his finger on, the old god made him uneasy. Setting aside his feelings of unease, Gaius took a second to actually ponder the offer at hand.

There's no way he's being completely honest. Odin has a reputation for tricking mortals into doing his bidding and trying to get his way. Swearing an oath to him would be risky, possibly even dangerous, but it would be nice to have at least one pantheon in my corner. I'd bet my soul that the Olympians are going to be gunning for me now, and I don't doubt that there are others who'd want to try to attack or use me. Gods, I wish that old woman was here to give me some advice.

Gaius looked over towards Tala again, who was now staring at him, waiting to see his decision. It was then that Gaius had an idea.

"Alright," he began, "I'll swear an oath of loyalty to you."

"Excellent," Odin replied with a smirk, "Ms. Tala, if you'd please come—."

"No." Gaius snapped, catching Odin and Tala off guard. "I said, *I* would swear an oath to you, but my wife, and anyone else who I might travel with, are off limits. Those are my conditions, accept them or any deal between us is off."

Odin raised his chin and stared down his nose at Gaius. His single blue eye peered at Gaius, daring him to flinch, to cower, to fold. Gaius made eye contact and held it, tilting his head to the side as he did so. Odin had an intensity in his eye that could easily break most people, god or mortal, but Gaius' pride refused to allow himself to cave to Odin's pressure.

This needs to work. I need this to work.

They stayed like that for a few seconds, each daring the other to crack. Odin reached up and stroked his beard, causing Gaius to fight his desire to flinch.

"Fine, I agree to your terms, but you need to hear mine as well," Odin finally said after what felt like an eternity.

Gaius breathed a sigh of relief before responding. "Of course. Let's negotiate, I guess."

"I only asked two things. The first is that when I need you to do something, you drop everything you're doing and you fulfill the task to the best of your capabilities. And the second, is that you would never do something that could intentionally harm me, or any of my kin. Does that sound agreeable to you?" Odin explained.

"Fine then," Gaius said, holding out his arm.

Odin clasped his wrist and spoke a word in Norse, causing a red wire of arcane energy to wrap around their arms. The energy seared his flesh, causing Gaius to yelp in pain. Odin's grip tightened as the god stared into Gaius' eyes, and seemingly his soul.

Gaius forced himself to stare back, breathing heavily through the pain that coursed through his arm. It was only a few seconds, but for Gaius it felt like an eternity. The line faded away, leaving Gaius' arm scarred from the wrist to the elbow. He looked at it in confusion, then turned his questioning gaze to Odin.

"The ability to damage or mark a soul is not unique, what scared everyone was the fact that you could do it somehow," Odin's explanation was quick and sweet as he saddled his steed.

"That hurt so much," Gaius panted.

Odin chuckled before holding up his left arm. He pulled back the sleeve of his woolen tunic, revealing a blackened scar that wrapped around it. At first glance, Gaius thought it was a handprint.

"There are much more painful things in this world, young one. Be sure to take care of yourselves," Odin said before pulling Sleipnir's reins.

Sleipnir set off into the forest, leaving Gaius and Tala behind them.

Silly child, Odin thought, *You can't actually think you outplayed me, can you?*

Gaius and Tala stood in silence for a few minutes, before Gaius finally worked up the nerve to speak. "I... Um... I thought that you wouldn't want to be forced into the service of a god," Gaius began. "So, I decided to try and keep you safe."

Tala stared at him with a quiet intensity that caught Gaius' breath in his throat.

"That's the second time today you decided something life-changing for me," she commented coldly.

"I know... And I'm sorry," Gaius replied, sincerely offering his apology.

"Shut up," Tala snapped.

Gaius' jaw shut up in surprise, almost biting his tongue.

"I don't forgive you, and it's going to be a long time before I can even consider it. You destroyed my life, and the only reason I'm even with you right now is because of how dangerous you could be if left alone. I will not help you unless my life is on the line, and once we figure out what's going on I'm planning on regaining my mortality. Are we clear?" Tala strode forward and jabbed her staff underneath Gaius' chin.

"Yes, ma'am," Gaius replied, his voice quaking.

"Good, then let's get moving. We've got a long way to the World Tree and this is just the beginning," Tala replied, striding forward with purpose.

Gaius walked behind her, giving her space as he pondered his own thoughts.

If this really is the beginning, then I just hope things don't get much worse.

A hollow laugh echoed through his head, causing him to stop and look around. Remembering the advice of the old woman, he chose to ignore it and continued after Tala.

www.ingramcontent.com/pod-product-compliance
Lightning Source LLC
Chambersburg PA
CBHW030616310726
48979CB00003B/740